Mr. Darcy's

Compassion

Jane Austen Reimaginings 6
A *Pride and Prejudice*
Novel

Rose Fairbanks

Mr. Darcy's Compassion
Published by Rose Fairbanks
©2019 Rose Fairbanks
ISBN: 9781798066584
Early drafts of this work were posted online.
Several passages in this novel are paraphrased from the works of Jane Austen.

This is a work of fiction. Any resemblance to characters, whether living or dead, is not the intention of this author.

Table of Contents

Also by Rose Fairbanks

Jane Austen Re-Imaginings Series
(Stand Alone Series)
Letters from the Heart
Undone Business
No Cause to Repine
Love Lasts Longest
Mr. Darcy's Kindness
Mr. Darcy's Compassion

When Love Blooms Series
Sufficient Encouragement
Renewed Hope
Extraordinary Devotion

Loving Elizabeth Series
Pledged
Reunited
Treasured
Loving Elizabeth Collection (Books 1-3)

Pride and Prejudice and Bluestockings
Mr. Darcy's Bluestocking Bride
Lady Darcy's Bluestocking Club (Coming 2019)

Impertinent Daughters Series
The Gentleman's Impertinent Daughter
Mr. Darcy's Impertinent Daughter (Coming 2019)

Desire and Obligation Series
A Sense of Obligation
Domestic Felicity (Coming 2019)

Christmas with Jane
Once Upon a December
Mr. Darcy's Miracle at Longbourn
How Darcy Saved Christmas

Men of Austen
The Secrets of Pemberley
The Secrets of Donwell Abbey (*Emma* Variation, Coming 2019)

Regency Romance
Flowers of Scotland (Marriage Maker Series)
The Maid of Inverness

Paranormal Regency Fairy Tale
Cinderella's Phantom Prince and Beauty's Mirror (with Jenni James)

Dedication

To all the readers that had to learn to fall in love with themselves. You are worthy. You are enough. You are loved!

Chapter One

Darcy peered out his carriage window as the conveyance rolled to a halt before the coaching inn at his usual stop in South Mimms. To the east about twenty miles lay the town of Meryton, Hertfordshire. As often as he had traversed the roads between London and Pemberley, he had never before considered what lay beyond them. His mind had only considered the path before him and the duties attached to the destination. Whether at his estate or his London home, his responsibilities to family and legacy did not cease. Despite knowing Meryton lay only a few hours away, and with it the woman he loved, he would cling to his usual route.

Inside the tavern portion of the inn, Darcy grimaced when told that the private dining areas were full and his usual suites unavailable. His decision to leave London for Pemberley was formed suddenly, only hours ago. Easter with his sister in their ancestral home was a convenient excuse. Georgiana's companion indicated that she was recovered enough to see him. Traditionally, Darcy visited his maternal aunt for the holiday. However, he was now sickened by high society and anyone who kept their views. Waving off the proprietor's concern for his offence, Darcy sat in the loud common room.

He glanced around the area, unsurprised to see he had no acquaintances in the crowded chamber. A movement out of the corner of his eye caught his notice. The maid moved with too much grace; her gown seemed too fine to be the usual sort. Was she some fancy piece trying to sell her wares? It was unlike Cuthbert to allow such, but who was Darcy to interfere with a man's business? As the lady's movements and figure continued to interest him—and invariably remind him of a lady mere miles away—he cursed under his breath for the fact that he now compared every woman born high or low to Elizabeth Bennet.

What would his family and friends say if they knew of his obsession? The earl would glare. Lady Catherine would lecture and throw her daughter at him. Bingley would laugh, and Richard, his cousin, would suggest he enjoy the barmaid's enticements and be free of his physical longing—and possibly mental torment as well. Darcy had too much honour for such, however, and so when he waved her over it was only with the intent to order refreshment. Never mind the fact that her laugh at the table next to him reminded him too much of Elizabeth's, and he had relished the warm sound when it washed over him.

"What would you like?" she asked.

Her voice was very like Elizabeth's. Darcy kicked himself again for allowing her to make such a slave of him that his imagination could go so far as to hear her voice. Looking up from his hands, their eyes met, and Darcy's breath caught.

Elizabeth gasped. "Mr. Darcy!"

"Eliza—Miss Bennet!"

"Par—pardon me!" Elizabeth laid her tray of ale down in a clatter and ran from the room.

Darcy stared after her. Why on earth was she serving in a tavern twenty miles from her home? The Bennets had not been as wealthy as he or Bingley, but their estate was prosperous enough. Only financial hardship or extreme love could drive her to such a situation. Darcy knew the owner of the inn and knew the Bennets had no relationship to him, which left only the financial motive. Before he could think better of it, he was in front of Cuthbert and tossing several pounds at him.

"That maid—the one who just ran out of the room—"

"Lizzy? Pretty with big, brown eyes?"

Darcy nodded. "Yes, that's the one. I'm paying her wages for the week. Find another maid."

Several men around him broke into laughter and raised an obscene toast in his honour, but he cared not one whit. As he dodged puddles of ale and urine, he followed through the door where Elizabeth exited. Hearing sobbing down the hall, he turned and then crept up the stairs. His heart beat in his throat with every step. There was another reason she could be here, one which lay heavily on his mind. Wickham might have ruined her. Darcy ought to have openly declared to the world that man's character. He should have told Elizabeth the truth and warned her. Instead, his pride demanded he keep his failings private.

If Wickham had not ruined Elizabeth, she might have been raped by any man down below. He did not think she would willingly sell herself, but many men took no heed of a negative answer.

Elizabeth sat on the top of the stairs, her head buried in her hands. The sounds of despair and agony split through him. Darcy bent at the knee and placed a hand on her shoulder, intent on offering her a handkerchief and escorting her to the safety of a room.

Before he could speak, he was struck on the side of his head. The unexpected movement set him tumbling down several stairs, landing hard on one arm. Along the way, he reached for the railing managing to twist his arm in a painful contortion.

"How dare you!" Elizabeth cried out, followed a moment later by, "Oh good Lord! What have I done? Mr. Darcy?"

"Aye," Darcy moaned.

"I am so sorry," she stammered. "I thought you were a stranger set on accosting me..."

The pain in Darcy's heart upon hearing such words could be surpassed only by the pain he felt in his arm. He heard Elizabeth's quick steps and a snivel as she wiped her tears away.

"Can you move?" she asked gently once at his side.

"I think so." He made to roll over, and she assisted him. No longer lying on his injured arm, it throbbed even worse as blood rushed around it.

"We should get you to your room and call the surgeon." Elizabeth held her hand out to assist him with his uninjured arm.

As his hand gripped around hers, he noted the rough nature of her palm and digits. Mere weeks ago, they would have been as soft as any gentlewoman's. What kind of life had she endured since he left Hertfordshire?

"We can get to the guest chambers through here." Elizabeth opened a door near the second-floor landing where he had fallen. "Your room must be this way."

"I am on the third floor, actually." Darcy winced as each step sent a jolt to his arm.

"Very well," Elizabeth said in a confused voice.

That she seemed unfamiliar with the layout brought him some comfort. "Here, room six, I believe they said."

He knocked, and his valet opened the door. "Mr. Darcy." Stevens glanced from Darcy to Elizabeth rapidly before he, at last, seemed to realise that Darcy oddly held his arm. "Is all well?"

"It is not," Darcy said as the servant stepped aside so he could enter. "I have badly sprained my arm. Please, see if a surgeon is available."

"Of course, sir. The lady's bag arrived a moment ago."

Noting that Stevens dashed away rather than be present for the necessary discussion, Darcy shuffled to the table and chair in the room. He could be treated there, and staying away from his bed would likely help Elizabeth's sensibilities.

"I am so sorry, Mr. Darcy," Elizabeth said, blushing. "I will leave you and your...guest." She glanced around, and her eyes fell on her bag.

Immediately, she stiffened. "Just why are my things in your chamber?"

"Cuthbert must have needed the room. I suppose he has already found your replacement."

"My replacement!"

"Well, I paid him for your wages."

"You bought me?"

Darcy could hear in Elizabeth's tone her anger and surprise, emotions he thought would soon fade. However, he had not expected the look of utter anguish to haunt her eyes. "No, I paid the man for the trouble of hiring a new maid and secured you safe lodgings until I can deliver you to Longbourn."

"I will never go back there. Never."

Besides the anguish, determination lit her eyes. He did not doubt her. He only wished to know how best to help her and convince her that he meant to be an ally. Before he could think of what to say, however, Stevens arrived with the surgeon in tow.

"It is a nasty sprain," the surgeon pronounced upon the examination. "Your wife will have to be quite the minder to make certain you do not overdo. You should not attempt the carriage for at least three or four days." He smiled and looked at Elizabeth, who had folded her arms at her chest and glared at Darcy. "It seems she is up to the challenge, sir."

"Thank you," Darcy said in a cold voice to mask his fatigue and pain. "Will there be anything else?"

"Yes, take this tonic twice a day."

He handed it to Darcy, and the stench made him wrench his face away. "Is there nothing else I can take?"

"This is the best for allowing you to maintain functionality while alleviating the pain. Shall I show your valet or your wife how to mix it?"

"Allow me." Elizabeth stepped forward.

The surgeon nodded. "Certainly, Mrs. Darcy."

Elizabeth blushed and sent Darcy an angry look, but he could only think how very well the title suited her and about the feeling of rightness in his heart upon hearing it. Tavern maid...potentially ravaged...or not, he would not deny his heart or this serving of fate.

Elizabeth observed the surgeon and then escorted him from the room. Darcy noticed his valet had gone missing.

"Explain yourself," Elizabeth said in an angry tone once they were alone.

However, instead of launching into an argument as he had expected, she nearly collapsed in the chair on the other side of the table. She looked bone weary, and all her capacity for anger had fled faster than a dashed light.

"I was breaking my journey to Pemberley when I saw a friend—" Elizabeth arched a brow at the word. "We are friends, are we not?"

"I hardly know who my friends are or who to trust anymore," she murmured. "I thought I had no one left."

"Elizabeth, what has happened? How did

you come to be in this place?" With his good arm, he reached forward to envelop her hand. He sought to lend support and comfort. Instead, she burst into tears. "Come, you are overwrought. Come, rest, and we will speak later."

Elizabeth nodded when he pushed his handkerchief into her hands and allowed him to lead her to the bed without protest.

"I will sit and read while you take as long as you like."

Indecision warred in her eyes.

"Please, Elizabeth," Darcy said with the sort of gentleness he often used with Georgiana. "I hate to see you so distraught."

Although more tears flowed at his words, she kicked off her worn slippers, slid beneath the counterpane, and rolled away from where he sat. He heard occasional crying, but she soon slept.

While Elizabeth rested, Darcy made inquiries with Cuthbert. Elizabeth had arrived in South Mimms in early January with naught but a few coins to her name. She begged for lodging and was willing to work for it, although with her genteel rearing she was no natural barmaid.

After a few hours' rest, Elizabeth awoke with a start. She sat up straight in the bed, breathing hard. She was shaking, Darcy realised. He left his chair to come to her side, and she jumped at his movement, then reached for a pillow to fling at him.

"Elizabeth, you are safe," Darcy cried out while blocking the projectile with his good arm.

"Mr. D-Darcy?" she asked in a quiet voice. Her tone was fear and relief mingled while her face expressed bewilderment.

"Yes. Do you recall where you are?"

"I...I..." she trailed off for a moment. "I do." She spoke in a stronger voice. "Oh, thank heavens. When I awoke and did not recognise the room, I thought the worst had happened."

Suddenly she stilled, and her brows arched. "I do recall everything now. You—you bought me, and you intend to take me back to Longbourn!" She scrambled off the bed, this time reaching for a candlestick.

"Good God, woman! If you will pummel me, may I ask you to wait until my arm heals and we are both fully able-bodied?"

"Your arm?" Elizabeth's brows drew together in confusion as she lowered her weapon. "Oh! I had forgotten—but then the surgeon thought..."

"My valet has set him straight and maintained your honour."

"How is that possible?" Her shoulders slumped. "Not that it makes any difference. Elizabeth Bennet has ceased to exist for several months now. If anyone knew the truth, my reputation would be entirely shredded. As it is, Lizzy Smith the barmaid draws no attraction or notice and hardly needs a good reputation."

Darcy gaped at her. For one, she would

always draw attraction and notice. She was too beautiful to blend into any crowd. As barmaids went, she was the only one he ever met who bore signs of genteel life—and the only one who had not offered her body for sale. "Lizzy Smith?" He raised a brow and approached her side.

"My aunt Gardiner's maiden name. Smith is very common. I thought Gardiner would be too memorable, especially so near Longbourn..."

Taking the candlestick from her hand, their fingers brushed. He returned it to the position next to the bed and then led her to the sofa. "I understand you must have been through very much for me to find you in such a position. Come, I will order refreshment, and you may tell me how I might assist you."

Elizabeth stared at him for a long moment. "It seems you must have gone through many changes in the time since our last meeting as well."

"Why do you think so?"

"The Mr. Darcy I met in Meryton would never be so solicitous to me, and he would never take orders from me."

"And the Elizabeth Bennet of Longbourn I knew seemed to love her home and family very much. Perhaps looks were deceiving on both of our ends?"

Elizabeth dipped her head in acknowledgment and took his offered seat. He rang for tea, and they sat in silence until it arrived. Simultaneously reaching to pour, their fingers brushed again. Elizabeth blushed while Darcy realised his body craved those fleeting touches.

"Pardon me." Elizabeth laughed. "I am

used to taking on the office of the hostess. Since this is your domain, perhaps you ought to serve."

"All that I have is yours, Elizabeth." The words tumbled from his lips before he could recall them. How he wished he could leave them as they were or fully explain his desires, but the shocked look on Elizabeth's face combined with her earlier words meant she was not ready to hear his proposition. "As you are my guest, of course."

"Very well." Elizabeth smiled and resumed the process of making tea. "Thank you, and to show that I am not as ungrateful as I am sure Miss Bingley has me marked down as, I believe I have recalled how you like your cup."

She gave Darcy a cup with a pert smile. He was surprised that she could recall how he took it. He would have preferred to make it himself; he had yet to meet a lady who could get it quite right, except for his housekeepers and sister. Still, he would drink it without complaint, for her, and there would be time later to reveal the truth. Pressing the cup to his lips, he sipped.

Elizabeth sat back with a satisfied smirk. As Darcy set the teacup down, he chuckled. "How did you know how I take my tea?"

"At Longbourn, you would drink it without sugar and wince. At Netherfield, Miss Bingley would give you three scoops, but you never finished a cup. At Lucas Lodge, it was two, but again you had a hint of displeasure about your lips as you drank."

Darcy listened in fascination. If she had

recalled such details, she could not be as indifferent as she had seemed. "And will you enlighten me to your process?"

"I put the sugar in first." Elizabeth smiled.

"Very good," Darcy acknowledged. "How did you guess that would work?"

"A lady never tells." She grinned and then took a sip.

"Then I will take it for the compliment it must be to have Elizabeth Bennet know such an intimate detail about me that I have hidden from most others. I am afraid you have learned I am horribly picky about my tea."

"Only about your tea?" She popped a treat into her mouth, her eyes closing with enjoyment.

"I do not think I am so scrupulous about other things. *I* never complained about Miss Bingley's table, for example." He raised a brow in silent charge at her.

"Oh! You remember that do you?" She laughed. "Well, I would not say I complained either. Mr. Hurst merely asked which dish I preferred, and it would hardly be right to lie."

Darcy only smiled in response. He had missed this so much. Conversations with Elizabeth were like a breath of fresh air, a calming breeze on a hot day. One could live without it but only just barely survive. In London, he had almost suffocated from all the insipid debutantes thrust upon him.

When they had finished with their refreshments, Darcy cleared them away. "I believe we must have some conversation."

"Must we? I would allow you to choose the

topic, but I can hazard a guess as to what you desire to know, and I am unsure if I want to discuss it."

"Why is that?" He moved to sit next to her.

"Are you asking why I do not wish to speak of it?"

"If you will not tell me how you came to be here and why you refuse to return to Longbourn, then it seems the next most reasonable thing to address."

Elizabeth shook her head. "How like you! You want to be reasonable, and I wish only to laugh and avoid serious matters. Well, having acknowledged that I would prefer to avoid explaining the circumstances which brought me here, the only thing worse would be to explain *why* I desire to circumvent the discussion. In that case, I would much rather relate the details than my feelings. Was that your design?"

"Certainly not. I can barely keep my wits around you. I could think of no design to make you speak when you are determined to be silent."

Elizabeth looked sad for a moment. "You once accused me of only wishing to laugh my way through life. How I hated you for that charge! In my mind, I was perfectly rational. I could laugh at the follies of others—your pride, for example. But I was blind to the real evils of the world. To the evils even in my family. I was determined to ignore them and applaud myself for the effort."

Darcy remained silent during Elizabeth's words. He had not meant that Elizabeth was too flighty. He had disliked the conversation, but he had not intended to demean her. He would have to address that—especially as she said it made her hate him. He had not thought—had never considered—that someone as rational and sensible as her could feel so very different about his words than he had meant them. At the moment, however, there were more pressing matters. Wordlessly, he squeezed her hand in a show of support. He did not relinquish it, and Elizabeth stared at their joined hands for a moment before continuing in a hushed voice.

"I have paid sorely for my arrogant stupidity. You will hate me forever when you hear it."

Chapter Two

Elizabeth could hardly think for the distraction of Mr. Darcy being so kind and solicitous to her. The old Elizabeth Bennet would imagine some arch or witty reason for her diversion from present matters. She would have mocked his kindness. Even now, she was not sure if she could trust it—she had been hurt by so many—but she would not devalue it.

"The morning after the Netherfield ball, Mr. Collins proposed to me." Elizabeth snuck a glance to see how Mr. Darcy took the news.

"And after you soundly refused him?"

"What makes you think I would be so hasty to spurn his proposal?"

"You are far too sensible to marry such a ridiculous man. All his talk about his parsonage and Lady Catherine would never turn your head. You are not mercenary."

"I sometimes think it would have been better for everyone I know if I had."

"How can you say that?"

"Let us speak plainly, Mr. Darcy," Elizabeth said and determinedly met his eyes. "I do not have the luxury of being as rich as you. Longbourn is entailed, and I am no heiress. Many women accept offers of marriage for convenience and security. As wife to the heir of Longbourn, I would have been able to keep my family in the house. Now that office belongs to Charlotte Lucas, and she will have it far sooner rather than later, I fear."

"Can you mean—but is it certain? Your father will soon pass?"

Elizabeth squeezed her eyes shut as hot tears spilled down her cheeks. They burned angry paths of humiliation as they landed in her lap.

"I fear I have no other handkerchief at the ready," Mr. Darcy muttered.

No, she had already used his, and she had not had such finery or luxury in months. Suddenly, Elizabeth felt Darcy's skin upon hers. She held her breath. Was he taking liberties? Should she rebuff him? Should she injure him?

Soon, she realised Darcy was tenderly wiping away each tear with the pad of his thumb, the way a mother would console her child. He was caring for her. He was the last man in the world she would have expected it from, and yet, as she had been so wrong about everything else, it seemed very fitting that he should be kind and compassionate after all. She leaned into the touch, craving the contact and comfort. Soon, he would withdraw it, just as the others had.

"I hate to see you distraught, Elizabeth." His voice rumbled in her ear. "I cannot bear your tears. If I could take your pain, I would. I know only too much the pain upon losing a parent."

She had never considered that before. He was such a young man to shoulder so much responsibility, and it must have come only at the hands of his father's early demise. She had imagined him entirely unfeeling. However, her tears were not formed from tender sentiment at the thought of her father's passing.

"You are too good. Papa has no ailment of which I know. I simply expect it to happen given the other disasters wreaked upon my family in recent months." Elizabeth tilted her head up in defiance. "I confess I would feel nothing but relief upon his demise now." Darcy said nothing at first, and Elizabeth prepared for his rejection.

"Do you fear my reaction?"

Elizabeth felt her mouth dry and fiddled with her tea things. Darcy stilled her movements.

"My father died believing to the last that a young man who was everything vile and evil was charming and proper. I cannot explain the hurt as I witnessed my father prefer that young man's company over mine. To see him so deceived and injurious in the process." Darcy shook his head. "I do not know what calamity has befallen you to bring you here. I do not know why you no longer want your father's favour. However, I do know what it is to feel betrayed by a parent. I understand the feelings of relief that come when freed from that burden."

Elizabeth wondered if Darcy had ever said so many words at once before. He appeared more open to her than he had been in the company of his friends at Netherfield. She had thought she had seen him in an intimate setting there. However, she now realised that the man before her had far more depth and compassion than she could have ever dreamed—in truth than she had ever witnessed before. If this was what laid beneath the surface of Mr. Darcy, it might have been difficult for him to converse with others who could not understand such feelings or even mocked him for them.

"Thank you," Elizabeth said as she noted that her silence had made him anxious. "Your compassion is refreshing and, I admit, of necessity to me right now. I had not thought others could feel as I do." Elizabeth smoothed her gown before continuing. "I did refuse Mr. Collins. My mother was enraged and spent all day attempting to work on my mind. Papa supported me. Charlotte Lucas had invited Mr. Collins to dinner at her home, as it seemed best he should spend less time at Longbourn. A few days later, I was informed they were engaged."

Elizabeth sunk her head. "I confess I did not like her choice. I even attempted to persuade her otherwise, but she was adamant. While I was engrossed in my own little drama, Jane received word from Miss Bingley that she had gone to London to stay with her brother."

Here, she peeked up at him. Elizabeth had long supposed Miss Bingley fabricated an attachment between her brother and Miss Darcy due to her own wishes in that quarter. Elizabeth had also perceived that Mr. Darcy did not approve of his friend's attachment to Jane. He did look a little guilty.

"I do not know if you can imagine the scene, but the Bennet home was at sixes and sevens. My

26

mother loudly bemoaned the loss of Mr. Bingley. She was certain—we were all certain—he was about to propose to Jane. Her grief was more than I can describe. She tried to rally, but her heart was too deeply touched by him."

"I had not thought—I did not know—" Darcy stammered as he flushed. "Was she very hurt?"

"She changed," Elizabeth answered and choked back a sob. "She withdrew and became distant. She spent more and more time alone and lost all interest in her usual employments."

"I am sorry—"

Elizabeth held up her hand to cut him off. She wanted to finish her story and have done. He could examine his actions and say his apologies when she finished. She no longer cared; she no longer blamed anyone—not Darcy or any of the Bingleys. They could not have foreseen what came from their actions. "Mama was often indisposed as her two eldest daughters had lost suitors. She was angry with me—I had thrown Mr. Collins away. However, she was disappointed with Jane, and she never had been before. I think that is what weighed on my sister the most.

"Mama constantly complained, annoying my father more than usual in the process. He seldom stirred from his library, and she rarely left her bed." Elizabeth shook her head as remorse swept through her. "I should have done better. I was so blind and selfish! Kitty and Lydia relished the new freedom as our parents became less watchful. They would walk to Meryton and spend the whole day talking with anyone they would meet. Mostly officers."

Elizabeth took a deep breath and then delved into the topic in truth, knowing that once she began it would bubble forth like a rushing brook. "Lydia never seemed to grow close to a specific man. She appeared happy to have the attention of them all. She became the favourite of Mrs. Forster, the colonel's wife, and was invited to stay in their home where officers came and went at all hours. Mama insisted that she go since Jane and I had ruined our chances. Kitty demanded to come as well. Mrs. Forster was more than happy to have her, and in the end, Mama wailed enough for my father to relent. Mama and the girls had images of balls every night and being introduced to other colonels. Mary never enjoys walks to Meryton, and Jane seemed so poorly that I spent much of my time with her. I should have visited my sisters more often or asked after them. Perhaps then I could have—but no, I do not know that I could have ever made them see reason, no matter what my mother says."

Elizabeth looked at Darcy for the first time in many moments and knew she had made little sense. He did not seem annoyed by her poor storytelling abilities. However, he would be more than annoyed when he understood just how far the Bennet family had fallen and how much she bore responsibility for it. "About a fortnight after they had gone to Mrs. Forster's house, the colonel arrived in the middle of the night in great distress. Lydia, Kitty, and Mrs. Forster were missing."

A quiet gasp came from Mr. Darcy, and Elizabeth nodded in confirmation of his unsaid fears. "It was after a dinner party with only a handful of others. A few were invited to stay for cards, but the colonel was called away. When he returned, the others were gone. A note was found. The ladies had eloped with the dashing, young officers."

"Who—may I ask the names of the men?"

"Indeed," Elizabeth said and squeezed her hands together. "I believe you know one quite well. The men were Lieutenants Denny, Saunderson, and Wickham."

Darcy turned white but managed to gasp out, "Has anything been done to recover them?"

Elizabeth could sit no longer. Tears streamed down her face and her eyes were swollen, but she needed movement. "What can be done in such a moment? The disgrace of the colonel losing his wife to one of his own officers became much known in the area, and with her infamy came my sisters'. One of their friends suggested that marriage might not have been on the minds of all the gentlemen. We soon heard word from Kitty. She had made it to Scotland with Denny. Maria Forster and Saunderson accompanied her, but Lydia and Wickham...we had heard nothing of when I left."

Elizabeth threw herself into a chair and sobbed into her hands. "It's all my fault, as my mother never ceased to tell me. I do not blame myself for everything—that I will not take on—but I did distinguish Wickham. I thought him very gentlemanly. Lydia knew it. She was desperate to be above me in the esteem of everyone, and I also knew it was her sore spot. I nearly taunted her with it. My mother and father, while good and loving, do not always make the clearest choices for their children. I could see the evil that could happen in going to Mrs. Forster's, but I said nothing. I should have—I ought to have—"

"You are not to blame for anyone's choices but your own." Darcy interrupted her self-reproach with a firm voice. "You could not foresee an elopement, and even if you had, you are not her mother or father. Why should you have the slightest belief Wickham would not marry your sister? You had no responsibility to consider such things, and neither of your parents would have listened to you. I know this as a man who has the care of a much younger sister. I am her guardian and she does esteem me, but I am not her father, and she recognises that."

"You should not excuse me of believing Mr. Wickham." Elizabeth wiped at her nose and eyes. "You may not remember our last conversation at Netherfield, Mr. Darcy, but I do. It echoes in my mind constantly. I championed him and all but accused you of abusing him. I know now he must have lied. How you could have borne my gross impertinence, I do not know. Even now," she met his eyes with a cautious look, "you are far kinder than I deserve."

"Nonsense. Do not distract me with flattery."

The corners of his lips lifted up slightly, causing Elizabeth to mirror the action. "I would not dream of flattering you, sir. That would be a dangerous habit, indeed."

"You must continue. That cannot be all that happened."

"Indeed." Elizabeth's smile slipped. "You can imagine we have been shunned by most of the area families. Mr. Collins even refused to allow Charlotte to visit us. I have had no letters from her since she married. I assume she is well-settled in Kent by now. Mary no longer found solace in scriptures or music. Instead, she found it in her wine glass.

"One day, Mama had been berating me as usual. I could stand it no more. I gathered my pelisse and bonnet and set out for a long walk. When I returned, I was met with silence. I thought it a blessing. Mary had fallen asleep in the drawing room, and I was informed my mother had taken to her room. I was sure to find Jane upstairs; we still shared a room although Kitty and Lydia's was now available. There I found—"

Elizabeth choked on her words but pushed past the lump in her throat. "I found Jane looking lifeless. She was turning blue, and her breath was so shallow. I screamed for help. I cried as I pulled her to me. I tried shaking her. Mama came at the sound of my distress. Finally, her smelling salts were truly necessary. They revived Jane a little, and she muttered something about wanting to sleep forever. She asked for 'more.' More of what I could not understand until I saw the laudanum bottle on the table near the bed."

Surprisingly, the tears slowed at this moment. She had cried enough over Jane's distress. "I wanted to call for the apothecary. I desired a physician. I asked for our rector. I wanted anyone who might help Jane. I blamed myself that she had felt so hopeless and depressed and I did not know. I should not have left her alone."

Elizabeth paused a moment. She was exposing too much of her feelings and did not care to be so open and vulnerable to Darcy. Shaking her head, she focused on the important matters. "My mother refused assistance from anyone. No one could know the truth. Jane was too beautiful to be mad, and she would never wed if anyone knew. Everyone would blame Mama, and she would not have anyone say such things about her. It had been my fault. I was closest to Jane. Mama was always too ill to look into our lives. If I had married Mr. Collins or if I had not been so saucy to you, then Mr. Bingley might not have left."

Darcy visibly winced at Elizabeth's final statement. "I assure you, I quite enjoy your 'sauciness.' Did your sister recover?"

"Papa would not stand up to Mama. He would not call anyone to assist Jane. She was well when the others finally went to bed. After a few hours of sleep, she awoke and confessed to her attempt at taking her life. She was so ashamed but also thankful she survived. The next morning, I asked my father to find help for Jane or send her to London to reside with my aunt and uncle. He refused. Later, I walked to a nearby town and spent nearly everything I had on a hack. I left Longbourn without a backward glance."

Chapter Three

For a moment, Darcy could say nothing. He saw the proud lift of Elizabeth's chin—a gesture he had witnessed several times in Hertfordshire—and reconciled it with her earlier self-reproach. She believed he would reprimand her or scold her. Gently bred ladies did not leave their homes and all their protection behind. They did not travel without an escort. They did not shun their family, talk ill of them, or find work. Elizabeth was a survivor, but how many others might be in her position and remain the silent and dutiful daughter? How many might it drive to Jane's choice? He knew from his own sister the repercussions of concealing pain. Thank the heavens, Elizabeth might be saved such a fate by her bravery.

There was still much to say and understand. Instinctively, Darcy knew Elizabeth's story had more to it. How could Elizabeth be so friendless as to live as a barmaid in a tavern in a small market town so far away from London and Meryton? Additionally, he knew she must have had some reason to leave Jane behind. "How came you to be here?" he asked her. "Meryton lies on a different road."

Elizabeth blinked in confusion. "You do not condemn me?"

"Not in the least. I applaud your strength!"

"I would say you did not always find it so appealing, but I suppose you would rather me answer your questions."

Darcy did not know what she referenced. It seemed her belief that he would censure her did not rely entirely on her recent experiences. Instead of asking after the source of this belief, he nodded in reply.

"I made it as far as Ware and then sent an express to my aunt and uncle Gardiner in London. Usually, when Jane or I visit them, they will send a hack to Cheshunt, and then Papa only has to send the carriage halfway. I was already nearly there but almost entirely out of funds. I wrote to them from a carriage inn a few miles from there. I begged them to take me in and told them about Jane. My faith in them was so strong—I believe I loved them more than I did my parents. What was left of my heart broke when they refused. They had sent an express ahead and scolded my foolishness in leaving Longbourn. They were packing that very minute to take me back. They called me ungrateful and unloving. They declared I would put my mother in an early grave. They did not even acknowledge Jane's illness."

"Such things make some people very uncomfortable," Darcy said. "It ought to be talked about more." From his sister's situation, he knew no good came from silence.

"Unwilling to return to Longbourn, I spent the last of my money on a hack and then walked the rest of the way to this village. Here, Mr. Cuthbert had pity on me and allowed me to work for room and board."

"How long have you been here?"

"About two months," Elizabeth said, and her chin quivered.

"You have been through more than anyone should—betrayed by all you knew and trusted. My heart truly breaks for you."

Elizabeth looked at him warily. "Why should it? Why should you feel so much for me? Why take me in? Why ask all these questions?"

Suddenly, she bolted from her seat. "Oh, I have been such a fool. Has this made you feel mighty? How the Bennets have fallen; how Elizabeth Bennet—headstrong, impertinent girl that she is—has her just desserts."

She darted to the door, but Darcy reached it first. "Madam, I will not allow you to leave my company and face God knows what out there."

"I have been here months and have managed to keep my virtue intact, if that is your concern." She glared at him, tilting her head back to meet his eyes. "I have no reputation left to lose at any rate."

"I have no care for your virtue or reputation! I care for you! It is not safe, and you require rest. Your mental fortitude is at stake, which I cherish far more—"

"Cherish?" Elizabeth's eyes fluttered, and the tension in her frame eased. She now appeared slightly more confused than affronted.

Darcy led her back to the sofa. "It is natural after so many hurts to be wary of others. You do not know who you can trust, and I did not display much in our previous acquaintance to earn it."

"No," she agreed. "You did not."

"Allow me to rectify that now." He knelt at her side. "I will not return you to Longbourn. I do not condemn you, and I am not mocking you. Indeed, the story of your family concerns me, and I will speak more on that later. Allow me to assist you."

"Are you to be my benefactor now? I did not forget your high-handedness in ending my employment."

"I ought to have considered differently, and if you still wish employment after you hear my offer, then I will help you procure some honourable position."

"What is your offer?"

Darcy saw Elizabeth's hand grip the armrest of the sofa and felt her body shift to plant her feet more firmly on the ground. She was ready to dash away from him in an instant. It made his next words all the more foolish than if she were only a penniless runaway. Indeed, Elizabeth did not trust him and probably did not even like him very much. It mattered not. Once more, Darcy gathered her hands in his and attempted to put all the sincerity and emotion he could into his eyes. "I offer you my hand in marriage."

Elizabeth leaned forward and peered into his eyes before ripping a hand from his and placing it on his brow. "Are you unwell, Mr. Darcy?"

"I am not ill and of a perfectly sound mind, if that is what you are asking."

Pulling her hand away, Elizabeth leaned back in her seat. "Why would you offer me marriage? A man in your position must think he could have me for far less. An honourable man might suggest the governess trade or a lady's companion. I had thought perhaps you meant to give me a recommendation to some poor relative."

"I apologise if my offer offends." He awkwardly rose from his kneeling position and took a seat on the sofa. Clearing his voice and attempting to conceal his mortification, he added, "I do not have any relations who would require your services, but I can make inquiries."

"Pray, forgive me. I did not mean to seem affronted," Elizabeth said quickly. "Only think of what you have heard. It would be madness for any reputable gentleman to marry me."

"Your present circumstances say nothing about your abilities. I am not taking a risk on an untried servant girl who can barely write her name. You are a gentleman's daughter."

Elizabeth gave him an astonished look. "And I suppose if having relations in trade were offensive, that I have worked in a tavern means nothing at all to you?"

"As it stands, it does not sound as though you are very close to those relations."

"So having no connections at all is sufficient? The conduct books should include that as a method to ensnare a wealthy suitor."

"Be reasonable, Elizabeth," Darcy said and leaned forward. "Do not make me into a monster. I would have you even with London or Longbourn connections. Even Mrs. Phillips—even Mr. Collins."

Elizabeth gulped. "Why is that? You did not appear some great admirer of me in Hertfordshire. I am convinced you disapproved of my family and—"

"But never you," he interrupted. "I never disapproved of you, Elizabeth. If I did not appear to admire you, it was only through the utmost effort. I, too, have had revelations in our weeks apart. As much as you have faced hurt and betrayal, allowing you to see the true character of friends and family, I have also come to realise the depth of regard I have for a woman who I could not shake from my mind."

"Forgive me." Elizabeth shook her head. "Months ago, I came to understand that I must have misinterpreted you. I understood that Wickham played on your poor presentation in public and on my obvious dislike. I perceived that if he was the very opposite of what he would show Society, then you must be as well. I should not have brought up past hurts."

"You are avoiding the topic at hand." Darcy had noticed Elizabeth's breath hitch when he said he could not forget her. Even now, her chest rose and fell rapidly. She would not meet his eyes, but she was not adamantly refusing him. She was not fleeing for the door. She did not push him aside. Indeed, now she claimed to think well of him. He leaned closer.

"You will regret your choice. If anyone ever knew of my misfortune..." She shuddered. "You would be laughed at, and your sister would be shunned by Society."

"I am not so simple-minded that I have not considered such an argument, weighed it, and found it unlikely. Even if it were to happen, I do not care."

"You are too kind." Elizabeth twisted her hands in her lap. "If Wickham is the foulest man on the Earth and he hates you, then you must be the kindest, and he hates all that you stand for. You cannot marry me simply because you feel sorry for my situation. Compassion is no way to start a marriage."

Leaning even closer, Darcy whispered in Elizabeth's ear, "What of love, then?"

Elizabeth stilled and gasped. "L-l-l-love?"

"I love you, Elizabeth." He caught the tear that escaped one eye with his thumb and brushed it away. "I love you as the headstrong woman who argued with me in Hertfordshire, the devoted sister who walked miles in the mud and did not care if anyone censured her. I love the misguided miss who attempted to put me in my place in a ballroom, and I even love you like this—wretched and poor, alone in the world, and feeling unworthy of love. I did not know it when I first saw it. I did not know what that kind of love was—but I know it now."

Darcy's heart hammered in his chest, and he held his breath as he awaited her reply.

Elizabeth could hardly make sense of Mr. Darcy's words. His words on love should bring a feeling of pleasure; surely they were complimentary, but she sought to diminish his reasons for them. The logic ran false in her head. She would think to herself that his senses were addled, and yet he had wits enough about him to converse this long and offer her aid. She would consider that he had always been peculiar, and then another part of her mind would scold her for reverting to her past belief of him. Time slipped by, and she became acutely aware of her long silence.

"In such a moment as this, I do not know what the customary response is. I thank you for your compliment. I surely owe you gratitude for your assistance—"

"Gratitude!" he cried. "I do not want your gratitude!"

"I meant no offence," Elizabeth soothed. "Surely you know me well enough that you understand I would not accept a marriage proposal only out of obligation."

Darcy said nothing but dipped his head in reply.

"There are logical reasons to consider your offer. However, I still find there are more reasons, out of consideration for your welfare and even more since your recent declaration, to refuse. What happiness could there be if I am so selfish? For much of my life I have been accused of bringing misery to all around me, and in such a situation, I truly could."

"I have stated that I do not care for the opinion of the *ton*, and I will explain my reasons to you later, but I do not want them to influence your decision at the moment. Your heart is far tenderer than mine has ever been. I can offer you security and a sufficient reputation. I do not promise glittering balls or being the envy of Society. I believe you would not care for such things at any rate. Fear not, the name Darcy is well-respected and garners respect. No scandal has occurred since our last meeting. However, my eyes have been opened to the disgusting practices and hypocrisy of many of the *ton's* favourites. If they think less of me for marrying you, then I will not have one moment's concern. Surely the world, in general, is too sensible."

Elizabeth stared at her hands as she could not meet Darcy's eyes. "Such unequal affections cannot be the recipe for marital happiness. You will forever be hoping or watching—"

"Are they so unequal? You have confessed to thinking well of me. Allow me to show you my true nature—such that I did not do in Hertfordshire. I would propose a time for courtship before pressing for a decision, but there are no available rooms for you this evening and I fear for your safety. My honour and affection can offer you nothing less than marriage if you stay here."

Elizabeth furrowed her brow. "I could return to my old room."

"Do you really wish to do that?"

Elizabeth shook her head. The other girls she roomed with were friendly, but they often shocked her by bringing gentlemen back to their quarters. Her virtue was intact, but her innocence was long gone. She had never been assaulted but was propositioned daily, and there was always the possibility the next man might not accept her refusal. "No."

"I will not hope for more than you can promise to give, Elizabeth."

The urgency in Darcy's voice pulled on Elizabeth's heart. He so desperately wished for her to accept him, and she perceived a good measure of that was for her sake—not his. She had once prided herself on being sensible. For too long she had reacted on emotion alone. Mr. Darcy was a good, honourable man. His name would provide her with security and protection. She would never want for food or comforts again.

"I accept on condition." Her voice faltered, but the joy in Mr. Darcy's eyes at her words encouraged her to continue. "On the condition that we begin with mutual respect and esteem. I cannot promise to ever fall in love with you. You surely deserve my love, as insufficient a return as it would be, but I do not know that I am capable of loving anyone else again."

"You honour me." Darcy raised her hands to his lips. "Thank you, Elizabeth. You will not regret it." Squeezing her hands, he allowed her to return them to her lap. "Respect and esteem are the foundation of friendship, and I will not press for more than that or demand any husbandly rights."

"Sir, I will be your wife! Will you not—?" Elizabeth blushed. It was indiscreet for her to know of the actions of married couples, let alone speak of them.

"I know that you do not reciprocate my feelings. I will not take or ask for what you do not wish to give."

"I..." Elizabeth blushed as she considered what her next words would mean. "I do not wish to avoid the...ahem...experiences...of a married lady. I would not wish for a life without children. Surely if I am to bear the burdens of marriage, I should enjoy the liberties as well."

Darcy's lips twitched, and a smug look appeared in his eyes, causing Elizabeth's cheeks to heat even more.

"What do you expect are the burdens of marriage?" he asked.

"My parents never seemed to agree on anything. If my mother was serious in a concern, my father mocked it. If my father was serious, my mother could not comprehend why." Elizabeth twisted the handkerchief in her hands. Speaking or thinking of her family now made her nervous. "It seems they only married out of attraction, although I suppose my father believed it to be love."

"Is that what has worried you about my offer? That I cannot discern the difference between love and attraction?" When Elizabeth nodded, he continued. "And does this mean that you are also attracted to me and distrust it?"

Elizabeth's face had finally returned to her usual colouring but flamed red again at his words. "You are not without charms."

"Oh, I am very much without charm."

Was there amusement in his voice? He looked as though he immensely enjoyed this. "You know you are handsome."

"There is quite the difference between thinking well of yourself and hearing of one's manly beauty from the lady one admires."

Elizabeth pursed her lips. "I did not say 'manly beauty.' I can see that my role will be to tease you lest you become too arrogant."

"I hope you will," he answered with real joy lighting his eyes.

"I thought you did not like it. Miss Bingley said—"

"Miss Bingley is often incorrect. I very much enjoy your method over her form of taunting. I have not seen you be uncivil, but neither do you feign approval or interest. When you dislike something, you are direct about it. There is no intention to unjustly ridicule or condemn." Darcy shrugged. "Your light-hearted way of teasing is a part of who you are. I would not wish for that to change or cease. It is a part of what made me fall in love with you."

Elizabeth sighed. He really could be so eloquent when he tried. It would not be an awful thing to be courted or loved by this man for her entire life. She believed he would always respect her. "Thank you."

"Now," Darcy said while leaning forward, "should I put your mind at ease about the liberties in marriage which you mentioned?"

"Sir!" Elizabeth cried. "You really must stop that."

"Stop what?" He chuckled and moved a little closer.

"Shocking me so I will blush."

"But it is such a delightful blush." He cupped a rosy cheek. "May I request something of you?"

Elizabeth's breath caught as she guessed what he would ask. Meeting his eyes, she subtly and slowly nodded.

"Except in very formal situations, would you call me Fitzwilliam, and may I call you Elizabeth rather than Mrs. Darcy?"

Inwardly laughing at her folly, she agreed. Hearing Mrs. Darcy falling from his lips and directed at her made tingles spread over her body. It felt foreign, and yet it settled in the pit of her stomach as right.

"Now, it is growing quite late, and we should get some rest. I will allow you the bed, and I shall sleep on the settee. No, no," he argued above her words, "I insist. I shall wait in the hall to allow you some privacy."

Elizabeth smiled her thanks, and he made his way to the door. Just before leaving, he looked over his shoulder at her. "And Elizabeth?"

"Yes?"

"I will claim that kiss later."

Immediately turning scarlet, Elizabeth noted the grin Darcy wore as he left.

Chapter Four

D arcy allowed Elizabeth a half an hour to go through her nightly ablutions. He had requested that the valet purchase some feminine soaps and lotions as he believed Elizabeth must have gone without such luxuries since leaving Longbourn. She did not appear unclean or unkempt to him. However, he knew she could no longer afford the sorts of products she would be accustomed.

Never again, he vowed. Never again would she go without. On the morrow, he would write to his solicitor to begin settlement matters. They would stop in London on their way to Scotland. There he would sign the documents and have all of that arranged before their marriage.

A part of him hated the idea of an elopement. Georgiana might feel it hypocritical, but they had no other choice. Her family did not deserve consideration even if the law afforded Mr. Bennet rights until Elizabeth's first and twentieth birthday, which, regrettably, was many months away. He could put Elizabeth up in some hidden location in London where her family could not reach her, but calling the banns would merely invite trouble. It would also promote questions in Hertfordshire. He could hardly imagine what story the Bennets had devised to make up for Elizabeth's abrupt departure. However, they could more easily cover a sudden romance and an elopement than weeks of courtship in London.

That the Bennets must have invented some story about Elizabeth to explain her absence, Darcy heartily believed. If her disappearance would only ruin her reputation, they likely would not trouble themselves. However, what Elizabeth did could reflect on the remaining sisters and whatever bits of good reputation they had. If they would not consider treatment for Jane's illness out of fear of judgment, then Darcy doubted they would want more attention brought to yet another missing daughter.

After they were safely married, Darcy would consider how best to remove Jane and Mary from their wayward parents. Finding Lydia would be the first goal. If they were fortunate, they might find Wickham as well.

On that subject, Darcy knew he would soon have to tell Elizabeth about his change in understanding of the *ton* and the shocking, appalling truth he had learned from Georgiana.

Knocking on the door to the room, Elizabeth called out that he might enter. Darcy knew from the volume of her voice that she must already be in bed as it was in the far corner, but he could not keep his eyes from ascertaining the truth. She looked adorable bundled up in the bed with the coverlet up to her chin. Soon he would call her wife and have the right to lie beside her.

Redirecting his thoughts, Darcy walked to the settee. A week's "rest" on it would probably cause more injury to his back than travelling would do to his arm. A week in cramped quarters with the woman he loved and would marry—that most assuredly was more dangerous than anything that could happen travelling with a tender arm.

"Focus on something else," Darcy mumbled under his breath.

"Pardon?" Elizabeth called from the bed.

Darcy squeezed his eyes shut and began to remove his coat. This was folly. He ought to have hired a maid for her and sent her on to another inn. What was he thinking tempting fate?

"Fitz...Fitzwilliam?"

"I had asked if you require anything else."

"No..." She sounded uncertain.

"Are you sure?"

"No, I think I need rest more than anything else." She stifled a yawn.

Darcy nodded and proceeded to remove his waistcoat. Shirtsleeves and breeches it would be. He could get no tolerable rest in his coats. His eyes scanned the room. He would need a quilt... Of course, the extra one would be on the bed. He slowly approached. Elizabeth had her eyes closed.

"Pardon me," he said, and her eyes flew open, then widened at his attire. "Might I have the extra coverlet?"

"Oh, certainly." Elizabeth sat up a little, the blanket dropping from her chin but still entirely covering her body. "I ought to have considered that and put it over there. I am unused to sharing a bed—" Elizabeth silenced and turned red.

"Think nothing of it. I am a grown man and can see to my needs. I would not expect you to anticipate my desires." At the moment, he most certainly did not want her to know the direction of his wants and wishes. "Sleep well, Elizabeth."

"Sleep well." Elizabeth gave him a nervous smile and returned her head to the pillow.

Uncomfortable on the settee while simultaneously worried about Elizabeth and overjoyed at her acceptance of his proposal, Darcy found it difficult to fall asleep. She, on the other hand, had quickly fallen asleep but talked and muttered to herself throughout it. Darcy was equal parts enchanted and annoyed by it. Eventually, he nodded off.

A floorboard creaked, awakening him. Who was in his room? Were they there to hurt Elizabeth? The floor groaned again; the fiend was near the door. They must have just entered. Springing to life, Darcy rolled and lunged at the intruder. Ignoring the pain in his arm, he grabbed at their legs, and yanked until they fell. Darcy scrambled atop the slender-framed man and pinned his arms down.

"Who are you? What do you want?"

"F-F-Fitzwilliam?"

Elizabeth's voice was breathy and full of fear but not from the far corner of the room. Belatedly, Darcy realised the would-be attacker wore a skirt and was a woman.

"Elizabeth!" Darcy pulled back. His eyes adjusting to the dark allowed him to make out her countenance. "Forgive me, I believed you were an intruder."

"Someone intent on stealing from the great Mr. Darcy of Pemberley?" Elizabeth jested, but her voice still sounded fearful to Darcy.

"Yes, my most precious thing." Darcy knelt at her side and assisted her in sitting.

"Oh? What would that be?"

He chose not to answer. "Are you injured?"

"Just a bump."

Darcy frowned. He thought he had defended his domain better than that. He stood and offered a hand to help Elizabeth. As she began to put weight on her foot, she yelped in pain.

"You are hurt!" Darcy sunk back on his haunches. "It is my fault!"

"No," Elizabeth hastened to say. "It was mine." She shivered.

"Let us get you back to the bed. Should I send for the apothecary?"

"No, it is not my first twisted ankle. Elevation and rest will sort it out. However, I do not think I can stand."

"I shall carry you."

"Your arm!"

"It is a short distance." Darcy began to slide one arm under Elizabeth's legs. "Wrap your arms around my neck." Elizabeth's nearness was making it hard for him to concentrate and distracted him from any pain he should feel from the effort. Elizabeth clung to him, most likely to spare more weight on his arm. "Relax, my love."

Darcy slowly made his way across the room, barely able to see the next step before him. He ought to have found a candle before he played the hero. The excitement wore off, and his arm began to throb. Sweat beaded on his forehead as he prayed the bed would appear.

Suddenly, his arm gave out, and Elizabeth, who had loosened her grip too much, slipped from his hold. She landed with a flop on the bed and let out a moan as her ankle jostled. Darcy, who had been in mid-motion, bumped against the bed and fell atop her, landing on his arm. Gritting his teeth against the pain, he began to pull back.

"We are a pair, are we not?" Elizabeth laughed.

"Indeed." Darcy chuckled. Stumbling in the darkness, he lit a candle before gathering several cushions from the settee. As he had expected, she blushed as he placed them under her leg. Then he sat next to her on the edge of the bed. "Why were you at the door? From where did you return?"

"I had not gone anywhere." Elizabeth stared at her hands. "I was leaving."

"Leaving?" Darcy's tone sounded incredulous but could not convey his deeper feelings. "You would leave me?"

"I...I..." Elizabeth sobbed into her hands for a moment. As suddenly as the outburst began, she ended it. "No, no more of that. I will not resort to tears every time I am unhappy or uncomfortable."

"I applaud the notion." He waited for her to answer as honestly as she always had.

"I awoke and was startled by my surroundings again. However, I recalled where I was before I left the bed. I panicked for an entirely different reason. Connection to me would only bring you and your family name ruin. I could not bear to cause you such unhappiness."

"And leaving me without a word or a note, having me fear for your safety and wonder where you were with no money and not even your meagre belongings would have helped? After telling you of my love? After agreeing to be my wife?" Darcy frowned. He did love Elizabeth, but he would not encourage this sort of behaviour and mindset. "No. That is not why you left. It had nothing to do with me. You know why you tried to leave."

Elizabeth swallowed and nodded. "I do."

"I do not approve of your momentary lapse in judgment. However, my fear and anger do not diminish the love I have for you even if you make foolhardy decisions."

Seemingly emboldened by his words, Elizabeth raised her chin. "I intended to leave because I think I deserve nothing. I should live in squalor and be friendless. Your generosity and love are so foreign to me that I would rather go back to the struggle I know than accept what you offer. I do not know what I was thinking; it sounds so ridiculous now."

"It is ridiculous but not without justness. You have been terribly wronged and betrayed by those dearest to you. Rather than blame them, you have turned on yourself, and I am too new to have earned your trust." He glanced at her foot. "It seems we have an additional reason to stay now and become better acquainted." Darcy stood. "I suppose I do not have to worry about any repeat attempts."

"No, indeed," Elizabeth said with a smirk.

"Good night again." He bowed, wincing at the effort, and took one step away before Elizabeth said his name. "Yes?"

"I will not banish you to the settee after your efforts this evening. Would you...that is... you should..." Elizabeth threw her hands over her face but could not hide the redness from peeking through.

"What is it you are suggesting?"

"I can only say this if I do not look at you as well," she said as her voice was muffled by her hands. "You should sleep in the bed."

"No," Darcy said and began to take another step.

"Would you? That is, would you for me? Twice now, I have awoken afraid of my surroundings."

"Will not a man in your bed alarm you more?"

"Perhaps," Elizabeth said as she continued to cover her scarlet face. "But if I wake you, then you might speak and calm me before I do anything rash. Eventually, I will have to remember you and everything that has passed this day."

Indecision warred in Darcy. Lying next to Elizabeth would be a dangerous decision. He did not hesitate out of fear of his actions. He would never force himself on her or seduce her. His thoughts, however... Darcy had yet to master them. Yet she looked so fragile and in need of his care. He would put himself through hell for her.

Wordlessly, Darcy walked to the other side of the bed and climbed in. Mere inches from him, he felt Elizabeth's body relax and heard her sigh.

"Good night, Elizabeth."

"Good night, Fitzwilliam," she replied.

Elizabeth nestled against the warmth at her side. She had never been warmer in a bed. Nor had it ever smelled so inviting—different from Jane's rose water. The scent was earthy and manly. The thought awakened her other senses.

Someone held her close to them. Strong arms—a man's arms. And yet Elizabeth felt none of the fear that she had the night before upon awakening in a strange room. Slowly waking, her memory returned. Mr. Darcy—Fitzwilliam as he asked to be called—was the man holding her.

All her life, she had thought such intimacy with a man before marriage was unpardonable. Indeed, she could hardly imagine being this close to a man after marriage and merely had to take it on good authority that loving her husband would create the desire. She had guarded her virginity in the last weeks when giving it up would have been far easier and given her some luxury. Now within a matter of days, she would be offering it to Mr. Darcy, and she did not tremble in fear at the thought.

When Elizabeth considered all the other gentlemen of her acquaintance who might have found her and offered their hand in marriage to rescue her, she had to concede that Mr. Darcy was the only one she would feel this—whatever this was—about.

"Are you awake?" he whispered against her forehead.

"Mmm," she said and took a deep inhale from where her head rested above his heart. A steady beat resounded in her ear. Slowly, she lifted her head to meet Darcy's eyes. The affection in them astounded her.

"You are so beautiful," he said and tenderly caressed one cheek.

"I must be a mess," Elizabeth said and self-consciously touched her hair.

Darcy caught her hand and kissed it. "You are stunning. I have envisioned this so often. I never thought it would be possible...and yet you are lovelier than any of my visions."

"You have thought of me—of this?" Elizabeth blushed.

Darcy chuckled. "Very often...countless times a day." He squeezed her gently. "The dream pales in comparison to reality. I really have you here in my arms!"

Elizabeth returned his smile, as uncomfortable as she was with such unabashed enthusiasm.

Darcy's hand slid up to her cheek. Cupping it, he met her eyes and earnestly asked, "May I kiss you?"

Elizabeth's breath hitched and her lashes fluttered, but she awkwardly nodded her consent. Slowly, Darcy leaned his head forward until their lips just brushed. His were soft and smooth. It was more exquisite than Elizabeth had ever dared imagine. She sighed against his mouth before pulling back.

Darcy groaned in what Elizabeth believed was appreciation and pulled her closer, fusing their lips to one another. For a moment, she felt his body tense, his grip around her tighten. Elizabeth raised her free arm and returned the gentle pressure she felt around her waist. Suddenly, Darcy rolled away, breathing hard and flinging an arm over his eyes.

"Did I—did I do something wrong?" Elizabeth asked. "Are you displeased?"

Darcy rolled to face her. "The only thing which displeases me about our kiss is that my desires are at odds with my honour."

Elizabeth furrowed her brow. New as she was to the ways of carnal temptations, she did not fully comprehend what he meant.

Smoothing the deep lines on her forehead, Darcy chuckled. "Do you know what usually happens when a man and woman share a bed?"

Blushing profusely, Elizabeth nodded. "The girls I roomed with sometimes brought men back with them. I would leave the room, but one time I came in unannounced..." Oh...he wanted to do that? Elizabeth admitted that the man she had witnessed seemed well-pleased, if pained. Her friend appeared less so, but she certainly brought men back too often to hate the experience.

"Ah..." He glanced away uncomfortably. "What you saw and were exposed to was something no gentlewoman should ever see and most never know."

"I know giving your virtue to a man other than your husband is wrong—but would they not experience the act itself? I confess I never thought Molly and Susie so wicked and yet..."

"I sometimes forget how sheltered ladies are." Something like regret emitted from his eyes. "A married lady enjoys her husband's... ah...affections from marital duty, a desire for children, and, I hope, genuine care and devotion. As such, the physical experience would be different than for someone who does it as an exchange of money."

"You mean..."

"Yes, my dear." He nodded. "It is not so unusual for women of little means to offer such services, especially at an inn. Nor is it out of the ordinary for men to take advantage of releasing their desires with any comely and willing woman."

Elizabeth frowned. Did she have the courage to ask the question that burned on her tongue? The thought of Darcy with another woman brought an ache to her heart and made her eyes sting with unshed tears. Yet why should it? She did not love him and had no right to feel possessive.

"What concerns you?" he asked patiently.

Elizabeth sucked in a deep breath. She could not explain all of it to him. Would she ever meet his past lovers? Were they indeed in the past, or would he continue such things? The chance for embarrassment would be very high. She had heard whisperings of kept women before. Did he have a favourite—one who would compete with her to be first in his affections? Or were they meetings with strangers? Out of the hundreds of questions she had, she focused on the one that mattered the most. "Have you?"

"No." He grinned when she sighed in relief. "I never liked the hypocrisy that a man might do what he will while a woman would be condemned if she acted the same way. Besides, there are diseases from such acts."

"And you will never?"

"No, I will never take to another woman's bed—even if you never welcome me."

Elizabeth had not thought such a conversation—awkward as it had been—would make her admiration for Darcy grow, but his frank and honest way of talking, his vow of fidelity even without relief for his feelings, affected her deeply.

"Elizabeth?"

She focused her eyes on the man she would marry.

"You should know, however, if we do ever join it will be very different from what you have seen. Pleasure is not one-sided and is a hundred-fold when both are in love."

Before Elizabeth could fully understand what he meant, he sat up.

"Let us begin our day. How is your ankle? I have been thinking, and perhaps one of the maids here might assist you in your toilette."

Elizabeth gave her consent, and he left to speak with Cuthbert, leaving her alone with muddled thoughts and an aching coldness as his heat dissipated from the bed.

Chapter Five

On Cuthbert's recommendation, Darcy obtained a maid named Molly, who Elizabeth knew well, to assist her a few times during the day. Molly could not devote all her time to it, for there was no future position Darcy could offer her in the household. A tavern maid did not have the skills to be a lady's maid or an upstairs maid. If she had a known history of occasional prostitution, he did not wish to offer her a place in the kitchen. That was the cook's domain, and she had firm opinions about her help. Additionally, this maid could potentially earn more at the tavern. Finally, it also would not do for Mrs. Darcy to be friendly with a scullery maid.

Returning with Molly in tow, Darcy saw to his own ablutions in his valet's room. "I apologise for intruding on your privacy, Stevens," he said to the man.

"It is no imposition, sir. Few men in my position would have their own room in any case."

"True, but I feel as though you count on that time and space to yourself."

"Truthfully, sir, I spend much of my free time below stairs."

"Do you, indeed?"

"I do. I do not crave solitude the way in which you do."

"Would you prefer to room with strangers?"

"Room with them, no." Stevens made a displeased face. "However, speaking with them, observing them, that is an enjoyable way to pass the time."

"I believe you have that in common with the future Mrs. Darcy."

"Indeed! My congratulations, sir."

"You do not look surprised," Darcy observed as the man continued to shave his face.

"You have never invited another woman to your room."

"True, but you could hardly expect me to propose to a tavern maid, I hope. I would rely on you to bring me back to my senses."

Stevens laughed. "I could hardly imagine that ever being the case. As it happens, I recall Miss Elizabeth Bennet from our time in Hertfordshire. I had thought then you might have a tendre for her."

"Is that so?"

"Yes, you alternately wore a grin or a deep frown after interactions with her when she visited her ill sister."

"I did not know I was so transparent."

"Perhaps only to the man who has made a study of your every expression lest I give you a scar for distinction." He smirked.

Darcy laughed in response as Stevens' hands hovered above his face. Returning to a neutral expression, Darcy said, "You said nothing."

"You said you relied on me to talk you into your senses. You did not seem on the verge of any rash decision. At the time, I would have thought her inappropriate to be your bride, but that was before this winter." His hands paused again, anticipating Darcy's next change in countenance.

A frown came forward without thought, and Darcy's brows contracted, bringing deep lines between them.

"It was a rough winter, sir. I had thought you were heartsick when we left Hertfordshire—but then things seemed even worse until we arrived here. Now, I would not think to counsel you against marrying a lady who can restore your smile, no matter what her current circumstances are or why she is here instead of residing at the estate to which she was born."

For the last few days, Darcy had managed to mostly put out of his mind the deep sorrow and rage he felt at Georgiana's latest confession. Deciding it best to return the conversation to the subject he had intended to introduce, he said, "Very wise. I trust you will not explain our reunion to the others at Pemberley or Darcy House."

"Never, sir."

"I must discuss matters with Elizabeth, but we will be altering our plans. We must still go to London—but will not stop at the house or spend the night, if we can help it. Then, our route must alter towards Scotland."

Stevens nodded. "I will arrange it."

"Perhaps some inns we do not stay at—smaller towns."

Darcy hoped not to meet with any acquaintances. If he were unknown at the inn, they could feign a marriage already existed between them. They could not avoid news of their elopement spreading. Oh, he could use his money and clout to fabricate a wedding. He could pay some clergyman to say he performed a marriage and they married by special licence. However, Darcy had better scruples than that and would not ask a rector to lie. The more significant problem was concealing that Elizabeth worked as a tavern maid. He did not care if they thought the marriage inappropriate and presumed he married too low, whether it be the daughter of a country squire or a lady in reduced circumstances. The problem was that many would assume her working in a tavern meant she had also prostituted herself.

Satisfied with his looks, Darcy left his valet's room and approached the chamber he shared with Elizabeth. Before knocking, he could hear the friendly tones of Elizabeth and Molly chatting. Yes, the faster they were separated, the better.

"Lud! Look at yourself. Fit as a princess!" Molly laughed.

"It is not like that," Elizabeth insisted. "He wants to marry me."

"Oh, that is what they all say, dearest."

Darcy frowned at the maid's insinuation.

"He is an honourable gentleman. I know he means it."

Elizabeth always could stand up for herself. What a pleasure it was to hear her stand up for him.

"How can you know that? The minute he saw ya, he bought ya."

"No," Elizabeth said firmly. "We knew each other before—"

"Before what?"

"Before I came here."

"So you were a fancy piece, then? Came on hard times?"

"How often do I have to tell you that I was never in that line of work?"

"Perhaps if you would tell me more about what you did do before, I wouldn't have to fill in the blanks myself."

Darcy did not like the direction of the conversation. The maid was too impertinent by half. Elizabeth might not recognise it, but there were all the signs that the maid was more interested in information she could use to blackmail them than she was in friendship. Darcy knocked on the door, interrupting their conversation.

Elizabeth called for him to enter. A sense of relief washed over him. He had not realised it before, but he had been anxious while separated from her. She was still here, in his room, safe and well.

"Thank you for your help, Molly," Elizabeth said with a friendly wave.

"Thank you for your services," Darcy said and dropped a coin into her waiting hand. "We will consider you again in the future."

"But I thought—"

"That will be all." Darcy opened the door, and after a glance at Elizabeth, the maid left.

"Why did you dismiss her like that?" Elizabeth twisted in her seat to glare at him.

"Be careful what you say to her and others."

"I am careful." Elizabeth harrumphed and folded her arms across her chest. "She does not know my real name. I have never told anyone about my past."

"She seemed most curious about it."

"She was just being friendly."

"It seemed like more than that to me," Darcy said as he settled into the chair next to the settee where Elizabeth rested with her leg propped up. "I do not know her as you do, so it is natural for me to be more cautious."

Elizabeth raised her brows. "But you have the right to overrule me and be rude whenever you choose? Some marriage this will be."

"I am looking out for your interests," Darcy insisted.

"What harm could come from her knowing about my past? If she blackmails us, refuse her. The most she can do is whisper rumours to whoever passes through this place—which, you may have noticed, does not typically include anyone from the *ton*. What about all your talk on no longer caring what Society said about me?"

"Forgive me." Darcy dropped his head. "You are correct. I have said that, and I mean it. I have learned to be on edge and worry about blackmail more than the usual person, and it has prejudiced me against others."

"And?" Elizabeth raised her brows.

"And...and I will hope to do better in the

future. I do not mean to overrule you. There are times, however, when we must discuss matters, and I might disagree with you."

"There's a shock," Elizabeth said with a grin.

"That we might disagree?"

"Oh, that is a given." She laughed. "No, that you apologised and spoke to the heart of the matter."

"I am incapable of doing anything else," Darcy said while relaxing in the chair. "I cannot make small talk or talk around things. I prefer a direct approach."

"And what of your ability to apologise?"

His lips twitched. "Of that, the ladies in my life are seeing to my education."

"Ladies?" Elizabeth's brow furrowed. "Oh, your sister. Well, I have never had a brother, but I know there are many things which might annoy any sister. I would expect a brother not to be very different from another sister about that."

It went far more than a mere annoyance, but he did not wish to shatter Elizabeth's quaint image of the Darcy siblings just yet. "What would you like to do today?"

"Well, with your sore arm and my twisted ankle, I think we ought to attempt flying to the moon. Once there, I will hike all over it."

Darcy could not contain his laughter. Elizabeth joined in for a moment and then sobered.

"Will you tell me why you think so meanly of London Society now?"

Pain seared Darcy's heart. He knew he must speak with her about it, but not yet. "Would you mind if we wait until this evening? Perhaps I may read aloud until then."

"You do not have to entertain me." Elizabeth smiled. "Surely you have other things to do. I recall a lady once observing that you must have a great many letters of business to write."

Darcy's lips lifted in a slight smile. "I had thought you were paying more attention to that conversation than to your book."

"I suppose that must mean Mr. Bingley's library needs improvement. Your library at Pemberley, according to Miss Bingley, is vastly superior. But then, you tell me, she is often incorrect."

"Our library at Pemberley is astounding." The hint of a smile turned into a full grin. "I cannot wait to show it to you. Yes, Miss Bingley often exaggerates or invents matters, but I do not think it is possible to overstate how many books it contains lest you compare it to some academic place like the Bodleian."

"I should like to see that someday as well!"

"Your wish is my command. I will take you there, and anywhere else your heart desires—except the moon. I fear I do not have the capacity to take you there unless it is in your dreams." How he wished she would dream of him the way he imagined her. Waking to her in his arms had been exquisite torture.

Elizabeth blushed and fell silent until a smirk came to her lips. "I must correct you, sir. On the evening of your letter writing at Netherfield, I did not read a book. I was sewing and ignoring that for any conversation. I will own to it proudly."

"Ah, but you were with a book one night."

"I believe that was the evening Miss Bingley chose to list what skills an accomplished lady needed to acquire. Fortunately for me, it did not include too much about needlework." A strange look passed Elizabeth's face. "I did not think then that any of this would be possible. I was as certain of Bingley's regard for my sister as I was of my feelings of superiority of mind to his two sisters and even to you. I had thought you the most arrogant man in the world with your long list of ridiculous requirements for a lady. Now I am to be your wife."

Darcy reached for Elizabeth's hand and raised it to his lips. "If you examine those memories again, you will see that I only said a lady must be an extensive reader, and that was because you were holding a book."

Elizabeth thought for a moment before shaking her head and laughing. "You said that for me?"

"How could I not? I did not want to embarrass Miss Bingley or offend her brother by announcing that I would prefer you ten thousand times over her."

"I had thought you were mocking me. I had closed the book!" Mischievousness lit her eyes. "Ah, but you also once sat with a book."

"I did," Darcy agreed. "My sole intention was to ignore you. My eyes were often drawn to you, and I knew you had noticed. I did not want you to think you had power over me."

"Indeed, I did not."

"I understand that now, but at the time my arrogance and prejudice only allowed me to see the danger I was in."

"And did you succeed?"

"You know I did not!" Darcy laughed. "You must recall how I closed the book the moment Miss Bingley began conversing with you and bringing you to my notice. I could not resist."

"I do remember. I remember so much from my time at Netherfield," she whispered in a voice of astonishment.

Darcy's heartrate accelerated. If she could remember so well, then maybe she was not unaffected by him. "I hope you think of it with as much pleasure as I do." He squeezed the hand he still held.

Elizabeth shook her head and sighed sadly. "I do not think that I do. I was confused... Your behaviour, even then, seemed inconsistent. One moment you were speaking with everyone, then focused on me. The longer we conversed, the more it seemed you only criticised or argued. Yet why should you exasperate yourself so much? My mind was exhausted from forming half explanations. A request to dance was not a sign of admiration— it was a desire to mock me. Your singling me out for conversation annoyed, but then so did your ignoring me on our final day."

"I wish I would have behaved differently," Darcy acknowledged. "I was confused myself.

I was attracted to you more than I had ever experienced before. It frightened me, which is not something I think I had felt since a small lad. I told myself at the time that I did not wish to raise your expectations. In truth, I was a coward. Pray, forgive me."

"Two apologies in one day! I do feel like quite the special lady!" Elizabeth grinned. "It has long been my policy to think only of the past as its remembrance gives you pleasure. I had not thought upon those days very often for it brought little pleasure—especially since the changes in my life. However, now that I know they were your attempts at concealing admiration—and how very like you, I might add—I may consider them happily. No, I will not forgive you. I rather like my memories."

Darcy's throat tightened with emotion. The acceptance of all his quirks and facets was something he had longed for all his life. Leaving his chair, he knelt at her side. He raised both her hands to his lips and then caressed her cheek. "I wish I could explain to you how much I love you."

Elizabeth's lashes fluttered, but she spoke, "Can you not?"

"Words would fail me. Even if I were blessed with oratory skills, they would not be enough. The greatest poets of all time cannot describe the feelings that beat in my breast or dictate my every thought." He had long been attracted to Elizabeth, but this was far more than infatuation or mental distraction. His soul felt a communion with hers.

Elizabeth gave a breathy command. "Then show me, Fitzwilliam."

As his lips met hers over and over again, he did just that.

Chapter Six

They passed the remainder of the day by taking turns reading to one another. Molly came after supper to assist Elizabeth in getting ready for bed.

Elizabeth thought about what Darcy had said. Molly did not seem like she was trying to learn more information about Elizabeth. The maid did not ask any intrusive questions and did not mention any more vulgar things about their awkward situation. However, Elizabeth saw the sense in being circumspect and not trusting Molly too far. A part of her mourned the decision. She had a few thoughts that Molly could come to Pemberley with her. After all, she was friendless in the world. She fell asleep resigned to accept Darcy's opinion on the matter.

The following morning, Elizabeth awoke in Darcy's arms again. She sighed, and he stirred in his sleep. She had learned that he snored. She had not noticed the first night because she was so anxious. Last night, she barely slept. When she did, the noises he made were so loud she could not forget that she was in his chamber and to be his wife. Not that she could have escaped if she had wanted, thanks to her ankle. She gently flexed the joint. It grew stronger but would pain her to put any weight on it.

Of course, last night was not entirely unpleasant. When it was time to retire for the night, they lay in bed and faced each other. Her hair fanned over her pillow, and Darcy reverently stroked it before giving her a good night kiss. Sometime in the wee hours of the morning, his breathing turned silent, and she finally entered a deep slumber. Now she awoke in his arms.

Looking up at him, a soft smile played on Elizabeth's lips. She had thought he was handsome when they first met, but then he opened his mouth, and she let her prejudice continue from there. When asleep, he looked positively angelic. The great artists should use him as a model. Elizabeth had never seen anything so special about Michelangelo's David, but Fitzwilliam Darcy was a worthy specimen to be cultured from marble.

Redirecting her thoughts, Elizabeth wondered why she had been so quick to consider the worst about Darcy. Months ago, she had realised it was due to her vanity. That is why she believed Wickham so easily. However, that is not why she doubted she was worthy of Darcy's love.

She had not told Darcy all her tale. How could she? How could anyone explain the insecurities which festered in her? She was so new to considering how her mother manipulated everyone around her—most of all Elizabeth—that she could hardly say it to another. One day, he would see the truth. He would see all her flaws— and he would regret his choice. Would it be as unbearable as when her father realised the truth about his wife? Was Elizabeth destined to turn into her mother: taking offence at everything and shrieking for attention?

"How long have you been awake?" Darcy said sleepily.

"Not long," she answered meekly. "Did I wake you?"

"No." He stretched, seeming impossibly relaxed in her presence, and then clutched her to him with his good arm. "I cannot think of a better way to awaken. How did you sleep?"

Elizabeth did not wish to lie, but she could not bear to tell him the truth. Soon, she was sure, she would adjust to sharing a bed with him. "Do you know that I have not been able to sleep as late as I would like in years? Mother had strict expectations, and then I was working here..." Elizabeth shrugged. "How did you sleep?"

"Very well," he said and squeezed her tightly again. "How shall we spend the day? I think we may only have one or two more nights before we can set off."

Elizabeth drew back. "The surgeon said you should not travel for a week."

"I usually recover faster than expected. Come, let us prepare for the day, and then we can talk about our route."

Elizabeth agreed, but Darcy did not move. "Do you not wish to rise for the day?"

"No." Darcy shook his head. "I do not wish it. I would stay in bed with you all day if I could." He let out a long sigh. "I would kiss you, but I do not think it is wise."

"Is there a reward for being always wise?"

Darcy furrowed his brow. "I would hope never to be foolish."

"And is it foolish to assure your betrothed of your continuing love?"

Darcy stared at Elizabeth for a long moment, and she held her breath. Had she gone too far? Been too bold? Why did she desire his kiss so much?

"If a kiss would assure you of that, then I would give it." He stroked her cheek. "I worry about being too selfish, but then you show me that to love is to give unceasingly."

Elizabeth pondered his words, but before she could allow them to solidify in her mind, he pressed a light kiss to one cheek and then the other. Next, he kissed the tip of her nose and eyelids. His lips lingered on her forehead, and Elizabeth sighed at the sensation. Finally, he brushed his lips against hers in the gentlest of kisses.

"I love you, Elizabeth."

Darcy said nothing else, nor did their kiss turn passionate as it had before. Instead, he held her to his chest for several minutes. It was a new sensation for Elizabeth. She felt safe and cherished. If love were a tangible thing, it would be Darcy's arms wrapped around her at that moment. In his arms, she felt protected from all the outside world and even from the sea of torment in her mind and heart. She held back for a few minutes before allowing the emotional release she needed. Darcy seemed to understand what to do. As she sobbed into his chest, he simply held her and stroked her back. Now and then he murmured to her about his love.

Unused to allowing herself to feel vulnerable, the spell did not last long. "I am well now," she assured Darcy.

She was not entirely well and might never be. He offered his heart while hers had been smashed to smithereens. However, she was nothing if not falsely courageous, and so she pretended confidence as per usual. She would feel well and whole someday, she told herself and yet doubted every word.

Darcy left and called in Molly to assist Elizabeth. This time, Elizabeth did not need to remember Darcy's words to be circumspect. She was too deep in thought to chat comfortably. What she needed was activity. She had always been an awful patient and was unused to sitting idly, especially since working here. Darcy returned just as breakfast arrived, and Elizabeth asked after his usual morning activities.

"After breakfast, I tend to the morning's correspondence."

"I recall the number of letters you received at Netherfield. That must take considerable time."

"It did at first," Darcy admitted. "However, I soon came up with a system of prioritisation to manage it."

"I wonder you do not have a secretary to assist you."

"My father did, but I prefer to see to the task myself."

Elizabeth smiled. "That is just what I expected."

"I see you begin to understand me." Darcy returned her smile.

It reminded Elizabeth of Mr. Bingley's long-ago words when she had said the same thing to him. However, she was not prepared to discuss Mr. Bingley and wisely refrained from mentioning him. Soon, they would have to address the situation of Jane's aborted courtship, but Elizabeth was in no hurry to do so when she did not have two good legs to walk on.

"And you?" Darcy asked. "I have often wondered how you would spend your mornings."

Momentarily, panic welled in Elizabeth. Memories of Longbourn flooded her. The constant noise of her sisters, the agitation of her mother, the nagging feeling of just never being good enough. She clamped it down. No one needed to hear those thoughts. "I spent a great deal of time walking."

"You are too modest," Darcy said. "You had told Miss Bingley that you had an interest in many things. Or was that only a ruse to put her off?" He sat back and crossed a leg over his knee as he sipped his tea.

Elizabeth chuckled. "The subject at hand was books, if I recall, not walking."

"Have no fear, she has insulted you by calling you a 'great walker,' although you did not hear it."

"Happy am I to know that Miss Bingley's insults continue even when I am not in earshot. What a faithful acquaintance." She laughed at the other woman's folly. "I do enjoy reading, although

I often found Longbourn too noisy in the mornings to read."

"What sort of books do you prefer?"

He had tried asking her that once before, during their dance at Mr. Bingley's ball. She had refused to answer then, her mind consumed by Wickham. She had championed the man, and then he seduced and abandoned her sister. She had been so blind and stupid!

"I enjoy history," Darcy prodded.

Elizabeth sighed. He was trying so hard for her sake. He had done it at the ball, and various times while she had stayed at Netherfield as well. She felt the compliment of his efforts. "I have read nearly everything in my father's library, but what I most enjoy are travel journals. It seems impossible to comprehend that other places can look so very different, that people act so differently from us. I read their descriptions of the land or sky and wonder how we exist under the same sun."

"You have left Longbourn."

"Yes, but only to London. Before everything happened with Lydia and Jane, there was talk of my aunt and uncle taking a long tour of the Lake District. I was to go with them." Elizabeth shrugged. It was just the death of another dream. She hardly dared to believe in them anymore. She felt no pain when they unfailingly did not work out.

"Ah, I see." Darcy nodded. "You think of these other places while you walk?"

"I have always had a vivid imagination." Elizabeth grinned. "We might call it Oakham

Mount and its elevation nothing high, but I have seen the hills of Rome from there. In the green shoots of March in Hertfordshire, I have viewed the greenest fields of Ireland. A river might as well be the channel."

"Perhaps now would be a good time to discuss our route to Scotland, then."

Elizabeth gulped at Darcy's words. Leaving this inn would set her on a path she could not stop. How she had prayed for such an opportunity for months. She had always dreamed of a band of gypsies taking her in or a child begging for her to be its governess. She had never dared to think that Mr. Darcy would appear at this inn and offer her marriage. Marriage was not a possibility for her now. She had been conditioned to believe that it was always unlikely. She had sunk so low, her best qualities stripped from her. Who would notice her? Who could love her? She could not even like herself.

"Does it distress you to speak about it?" Darcy asked.

Elizabeth quickly shook her head and smiled. She would need to watch herself if she did not want Darcy asking more questions and learning all the ugly truth. The contradiction made her head swirl. She could not return his love, and yet she hated the idea of losing it. She felt guilty for fraudulently earning it. He was under the impression that she was good and worthy, and he could not be more wrong. However, she could not bring herself to tell him.

"Please, tell me," Elizabeth beseeched.

"I had thought we would go to Holyhead."

"Oh!" Elizabeth cried. "I had not expected that. We will not take the North Road?"

"I think it too well-travelled, and we do not want to risk anyone recognising us."

Recognising *him*, Elizabeth amended in her head. They would need to travel under false names. It would be no extreme thing for them to have eloped. The problem would be if anyone would determine their route. The world must never know that she had been Lizzy Smith the barmaid. Still, Holyhead proved to be intriguing. "Will we sail to Scotland, then?"

"Have you sailed before?" Darcy asked.

"No," Elizabeth replied as excitement built in her. "I also never thought I would have the opportunity."

Suddenly, she thought better of her reaction. She should not be so pleased that she was in this situation and forced to elope. They could not even go the standard route. She was selfish. Darcy watched her, a look of growing confusion on his face. To avert questions about her change in demeanour, she redirected his attention. "I did not think we could reach Gretna Green by boat."

"True, but an anvil marriage is the same anywhere in Scotland. We shall be going to Portpatrick. Have you heard of it?"

Elizabeth thought before answering. "My father's books were mostly about the locations he visited on his Grand Tour."

"I would love to hear about them someday. I had to make do with a trip to Scotland and

Ireland. Napoleon made travel too unsafe." He sighed. "One day, when the war is over, we will journey to the Continent. Where would you like most to visit?"

"I will be pleased to go anywhere," she said before quickly adding, "with you."

"Elizabeth," Darcy said as he enveloped one of her hands in his, "it is perfectly allowable to be selfish. I have no wish for you to defer to me over everything."

"Surely I have not. Do you not recall our arguments merely since being in this room together?"

"Indeed, I do. However, I mean about decisions regarding our life together."

"When I have a great opinion, I will share it, I assure you."

"Very well," Darcy said and released her hand.

He seemed annoyed. She could hardly imagine what frustrated him when she was trying so hard to be agreeable.

"Portpatrick is popular among the Irish for hasty marriages, the way Gretna Green is in England. We can be lost in a city with many strangers, and most of them do not stay longer than an hour or two. There is no reason to pretend to be anyone but ourselves or fear we will be recognised en route."

"Splendid." Elizabeth grinned. "Did you say it was near Ireland?"

"I believe it is only a few hours by boat," Darcy said. "You may even be able to see the coast."

"May we visit?"

"Certainly." Darcy's smile matched her own.

There, Elizabeth thought. And he had acted as though she were a shrinking violet. It was true that she guarded her personal feelings and that they often felt like a ship tossed about on the waves during a fearsome storm, but she was unafraid to state her opinion about things of little consequence.

"Now, I believe we have promised to read to one another." Darcy produced a few books. "Shall I read first?"

Elizabeth agreed but hardly knew how to occupy herself during his task. As much as she hated it, at home she would have at least had a work bag and embroidery. She needed something to keep her hands busy lest she allow her mind to wander and go mad. He read for about half an hour before handing the book to her. She closed it and put it aside.

"I would rather talk than read. Will you tell me about your sister?"

Chapter Seven

Darcy tensed at Elizabeth's words. He knew he must tell her the sordid truth about Georgiana, but he felt incapable. The only thing Elizabeth knew of his sister was Miss Bingley's praises for her accomplishments. He could not tell her about the very worst of humanity before she knew anything else about Georgiana. After all, the abuse did not define her.

During Darcy's panicked thoughts, Elizabeth seemed to scrutinise his expression. He supposed it was only fair after he had done the same to her. She was also hiding something, although he was at a loss on what it could be. She had already revealed far more shocking things than any other lady of his acquaintance probably ever would.

"I did not think it would be so difficult." Elizabeth chuckled. "Perhaps that is because I have four sisters to talk about, so there is always something to say."

Darcy smiled. "Georgiana is in nearly all of my fondest memories. She was born when I was almost twelve. Of course, I can recall moments before. However, they are far hazier. She was the true apple of my parents' eyes. They had long desired a sibling for me." He paused to laugh at the ridiculousness of his youth. "I had seldom seen a baby and was certain I would not like the imposter they were bringing into our home. I only knew they cried and smelled. What use did I have for an infant? We were too far apart in age to ever be friends."

Elizabeth nodded. "There are only seven years between the eldest and youngest of us. I confess that it is often difficult to understand the minds of my youngest sisters, and I am far closer to their age than you are with Miss Darcy."

"In hindsight, I believe I was afraid she would steal all of my parents' attention. The morning of her birth, my father called me into the nursery for a proper introduction. I peered into her cot, my hands resting over the edge. She was sleeping but suddenly awoke. Stretching and yawning, she looked positively cherubic. Then one of her tiny fists wrapped around one of my fingers, and I was utterly lost. I laughed to myself that I had feared her entry into the world."

"How sweet." Elizabeth sighed.

"Oh, she was still loud and stinky." They shared a laugh. "I would visit the nursery as often as I could, impatiently expecting her to walk or talk. The nurse had to explain a dozen times that it would take a months before she could do more than lie down, let alone catch up with me.

"Georgiana was born in July, and I began attending Eton that autumn. For many years, I only saw her on holiday. Obviously travelling the distance from Pemberley to Windsor with a young child was nearly impossible. There was another motive, too. My mother's health was ailing. I do not know if she never recovered from Georgiana's birth or whether there were attempts at another child. I know it was a slow and steady decline but not an illness. When I did return to Pemberley to visit, I was instructed to be quiet and not bother my mother. I devoted hours to entertaining my sister. This was especially beneficial to me as George Wickham grew more malicious each year at school. My father discerned none of it and instead found great joy in the boy's charming façade to ease his troubled mind and mourning heart. I am convinced it is this closeness which resulted in Georgiana telling me about her intended elopement."

Elizabeth's brows rose in surprise. "You mean he attempted to elope with your sister?"

"You should not be so shocked. You have witnessed his charisma, and Darcys are mortal after all." His tease earned a slight smile from Elizabeth.

"What is her temperament like? You observed my sister Lydia. She did elope with Wickham. Are there any similarities between the two?"

"Other than their age and susceptibility to Wickham's charm, I would not say so." He hoped it would not grieve Elizabeth to hear it. He did not wish to talk about her sister's failings. "Georgiana is shy. While she is not studious, as her preferences fixate on the pianoforte, she is well-educated in a variety of subjects and is adequate at them all. Is there anything else you wish to know about her?"

"Where is she now?"

"She is at Pemberley with her companion. I intended to visit her for Easter."

"Now I have ruined those plans!" Elizabeth cried.

"Nonsense." Darcy waved away her concerns. "I have written to her and explained that I have been detained. Some of our relations may visit in my absence."

Elizabeth nodded and fell into a momentary lapse of silence. He turned his attention to another book, as she still had the one he had read from earlier. She sighed and fidgeted in her seat.

"Are you unwell? Should I call in Molly?" Darcy asked after several minutes of the unusual behaviour.

"I am merely out of sorts with being laid up for so long. I cannot even look out the window."

Without another word, Darcy stood, dwarfing the distance between them. Scooping her into his arms, he carried her to a window.

"Put me down!" she cried. "You will hurt your arm and have a relapse, and then we will never be able to leave."

"Pardon me," Darcy said as he held her close. "I had expected your thanks. You did just say you wished to look outside."

"But I do not wish to be dropped!" She gripped his neck tightly. "Yes, I see, it is a square just like any other town."

Although she said she was through looking, she cast a wistful glance at the window.

"A chair," Darcy said. "I can place a chair here for you to use."

"It is not necessary. It is only a strange habit of mine that I would indulge if I could."

"What is that?"

"I enjoy watching others. I consider what is going on in their lives, what their reasons are for buying a certain thing or moving a certain way. It is as entertaining as we can get in Meryton with no theatre."

Darcy was unwilling to relinquish his hold on her and lingered at the window. "That man in yellow breeches. What story would you invent for him?"

Elizabeth looked at the man for a moment. "Why, he is courting, of course! See how he hovers at the window display? He is thinking of giving his lady love something but does not know if it will meet with her approval."

"Maybe he does not think he can afford it."

Elizabeth frowned. "That is far less romantic, Fitzwilliam. Common sense, such as income, never figures into these scenes."

"Do they not?" he asked. "Would you marry a man with an insufficient income?"

"No," Elizabeth agreed. "But then I would never allow myself to be courted by a gentleman who dressed as garish as he. Perhaps he would do better with Miss Bingley!"

Darcy laughed so hard at her joke that he did not at first notice the fatigue of his arm. When he did, he realised he had mere seconds to deposit his bundle. Striding back to the settee, Darcy almost reached it when his arm gave out. Before he knew it, Elizabeth was in a heap on the floor.

"I told you not to carry me!"

He crouched to help her up.

"I can do it!" she hissed as she gripped the nearby table for support. Her knuckles turned white. "Now, if you could assist me to the bed, I will remain there. No," she said, leaving no room for argument when he attempted to lift her once more. "Wrap your arm around my waist and help me hop."

Darcy did so and then arranged the pillows under her injured ankle. "I am sorry, Elizabeth."

"You *should* be." She glared.

He could not wonder at the change in her mood. She had confessed to feeling short-tempered and irritated. "Is there anything else I might fetch you?"

"Perhaps you could speak with your valet or with Cuthbert about something. Do you like ale? There is always plenty downstairs."

Darcy understood her meaning. All she wanted was for him to leave. He withdrew his watch. "I will return in a few hours. You are welcome to my books. I will arrange for Molly to check on you at two."

He brought his stack of books and left them on the table near her side of the bed. He hesitated to leave Elizabeth's side, but it was clear that she desired some privacy and space. He wondered if it would be different if she loved him, or if she would always need some distance between them.

Darcy spent a few hours in the tavern below, watching other men grow rowdier as they consumed Cuthbert's beverages. Men pawed at their women or a barmaid. How had Elizabeth survived this for months? Before that, she lived at Longbourn with all its noise. He tried not to take it personally that she needed some space from him. After they married, even if she deeply loved him, there would be a period of separation. During the day they would each have their tasks. There might be a time when he had to travel without her. Indeed, that she could be so independent was an asset. He would not like a wife who senselessly clung to him.

No, what gnawed at him was the way she avoided discussing what she felt about things. She had informed him of events, and while she cried, it seemed no more emotional than a journalist reporting the news. He could guess what everything she had gone through did to her, but Elizabeth seemed entirely reluctant to voice any of it. How he wished he could knock down the walls of her heart!

Someday, he told himself. Eventually, he would earn her trust. One day, she would know to draw comfort from him. All he had to do was prove his loyalty and fidelity. When put that way, he was assured of success, and it would not even be difficult for him, for nothing could end his love.

The sun was slipping low in the sky and dinner was being served when Darcy returned to the bedchamber. He found Elizabeth waiting for him at the settee, their trays already brought in.

She looked refreshed and gave him a smile. He took that as a good sign.

"I hope you enjoyed your afternoon," he said as he sat beside her and kissed her cheek.

"Indeed. I apologise for being short with you earlier. I cannot put it into words, but I am restless. I cannot abide being cooped up in a room for so long."

"Once we leave, we could arrange a time on each day to give you a satisfactory walk."

"You would do that?" Elizabeth asked as she prepared Darcy's tea.

"I would do anything for you," he said seriously. His were not the empty words of so many suitors. "You need only ask."

Darcy watched Elizabeth's reaction. Did she believe him? Would she ever? Suddenly, it occurred to him that if he wanted her to be more open, he ought to show the same willingness. They talked about light things while they ate. Afterward, Elizabeth read to them from the book she had discarded earlier in the day. Supper arrived around nine, and after eating, they prepared for bed. It was there, as Darcy drew Elizabeth to his side, that he approached the subject of Georgiana.

"You asked earlier about my sister, but I did not tell you everything."

"Do you fear my reaction? You should not after all I have explained to you."

"No, I do not think you will be harsh on her. First, I did not want to tell you because I did not want to sway your opinion. Then I did not wish to tell you because we seemed to have enough battles, and I did not want to add to your distress."

"Is it so upsetting then?"

Darcy's arms reflexively tightened. "I can scarcely imagine a grimmer subject."

For a moment, Darcy's thoughts were pulled back to the day when he finally heard the terrible truth from his sister. It had come after he had returned from Hertfordshire. He had left her in London after weeks of her being so crippled with depression that she could not leave her chamber or eat. She had refused to speak or accept visits from her friends. She shunned any mention of the pianoforte or music. It was not the tears Darcy had expected when he told her of Wickham's abandonment. It was as though Georgiana was empty on the inside.

"You care for her very much," Elizabeth said as she pushed a lock away from his brow. Her hand rested at his temple, and she applied gentle pressure in a circular motion.

"Before you, she was the only person I had left in my life to love. I idolised my parents. It took no sacrifice on my part to love them. Georgiana had never known our mother, and I think that is essential to understanding this story. When our father died, I became more than a brother to her."

"Was there no one else she could look to for a father figure? That is quite a lot of responsibility for such a young man. What did you know about raising a girl her age—or any at all—while you were not more than...?"

"Two and twenty," he supplied.

"You were not more than two and twenty. I suppose you had full guardianship over her?"

"No," Darcy answered. "A cousin on my mother's side was also awarded guardianship in my father's will. However, he is currently a colonel in the Regulars and has had little time to devote to his charge. Of course, by then the damage was done, although we did not know it. I am certain even my father did not know."

Darcy's throat dried as his palms grew sweaty. His heart raced and his belly twisted in pain, alternating between butterflies for Elizabeth's response and the disgust such memories always provoked.

"You may tell me anything," Elizabeth encouraged. "I have..." She trailed off as she wiped a tear, drawing Darcy's eyes to focus on her. "Nothing can disturb me very much. I am no longer the sheltered miss you knew in Hertfordshire. I cannot explain the peace that sharing my troubles with you has begun to give me. Will you not allow me to hear of your trials in exchange?"

Staring into Elizabeth's glittering eyes, filled with remorse and pain at least partly for his sake, Darcy was more lost than ever. He could never deserve her love. He might never have it. However, she offered him this moment. A moment of reprieve and understanding. A precious, sacred moment he had prayed for in ardent longing for months. He sealed her offering with a kiss, then pulled her head to rest over his heart. For one more minute, he remained silent, drawing strength and comfort from her touch.

"Father had a friend who would visit. After Mother died, it seemed he came more often When Georgiana was about five or six years old, this man became quite taken with her. I was just entering university, so I do not know how frequently he came to Pemberley. We were told his own wife had taken a lover and kept his daughter from him. He could exercise his right legally but claimed he loved her and could not dishonour her even if she did so to him. He knew, too, that it would grieve his little girl to pull her from her mother. Whatever faults the wife had, her love for their child seemed genuine. The friend mourned the loss of his daughter and my father pitied him. He was permitted to visit Georgiana in the nursery whenever he wished. He often took her on walks around the grounds. He lavished her with attention on these visits and brought gifts. I remember thinking she loved him more than us."

If Elizabeth could sense what he was about to say, she did not react at all. Perhaps she had more innocence about her than she claimed. Perhaps her loving heart could not imagine all the horrors of the world. For a moment, Darcy hesitated. He hated having to tell her of such ugliness. However, she asked for him to be open, and he now believed it a necessary part of creating trust between them.

"That man—that monster, I should say— was not treating Georgiana as a daughter as we had so long believed. He treated her as a mistress."

Chapter Eight

A gasp tore from Elizabeth's mouth, and she raised up on an elbow. "Do you mean he—? But she was a child! Why would he?"

"Some men have such vile hearts. I have learned we are not alone in this. It took years for him to develop a deep enough bond with Georgiana for him to...to consummate their relationship."

The first time he spoke the words aloud, Darcy thought he might pass out. This was only the second time, and it was hardly better. Bile rose in his throat, and he bit his tongue to replace the taste with blood.

"And your father never knew? No one knew? How could no one have knowledge of this?"

"Georgiana says it began when she was ten and ended when she started her courses. She started them late; for a time the physician was greatly worried for her. Apparently, that is not unusual in these cases."

"I suppose by that age she would not be under a very watchful eye of a governess or bound to the nursery as much."

"No, and he was always welcome to walk about with her. Do you understand? Most of the time she endured this hell was after my father died. When I ought to have protected her! I was too busy with everything else in life to notice. In the year after her courses began, he visited less and less. I had thought it was due to his aging. Georgiana's moods varied wildly, and I believed sending her to school would be for the best. She needed the company of other girls her age."

Darcy could feel the dampness from Elizabeth's tears, and his own fell on her hair. For several minutes, they said nothing to one another. Darcy allowed Elizabeth time to wrap her mind around what he had shared and consider any questions if she had them. He could not imagine revealing the truth to any other lady he knew. Something he had learned in the last several weeks was that very few people could accept such scenarios as he had just described. He was told that people often did not mean to be cruel, but they simply could not accept a reality in which children were harmed in this way.

"Is your sister well? I can only imagine..." Elizabeth choked back a sob. "I can only imagine such things would wound deeply."

"She is healing, at last," Darcy said. "I cling to the proof of her improvement. The experiences with her abuser confused her greatly. She hated him but loved him. She loathed herself. She said nothing of this to me until recently. I had not seen Wickham in nearly three years when he came asking for the living which was intended for him. He had voluntarily given it up after the deaths of our fathers, as he intended to study the law. I gave him three thousand pounds in exchange for his agreement to give up any claim to the church. He spent two or three days in the area before seeking his request, as though two days of good behaviour would make up for my ill opinion of him for the better part of a decade. It was all too easy for Georgiana to transfer her feelings to another man who gave her attention as a child but had more promise of returning."

Disgust filled Darcy anew. "I did not know about the abuse. It was inconceivable to me that our friend would be so evil or that such atrocity even existed. Wickham, however, I knew and distrusted. Still, I did not enlighten my sister about him. About a year later, she completed her schooling, and I hired a companion for her. They asked to holiday in Ramsgate. I did not know the companion had previously known Wickham, who arrived soon after them. I unexpectedly arrived a day or two before their intended elopement."

Elizabeth shook in his arms as sobs racked her.

"I am very sorry, my love. If I had exposed Wickham's actions against my family, I could have prevented his wounding yours."

"No," Elizabeth cried. "No, you could not. Kitty eloped with another man. Lydia would have been just as eager to marry anyone—or especially any soldier. She was desperate to take precedence and get away."

"Perhaps," Darcy said as he stroked Elizabeth's back. "However, she probably would have chosen a man who would actually marry her. I mean no insult, but I would wager Wickham would not be tempted to the altar by a woman with less than twenty thousand pounds. If I had any way of supposing she had a tendre for him—"

"Exactly," Elizabeth said. "You never would have suspected it. You cannot be held responsible for the thoughts of a silly girl." She searched his eyes. "How did you learn all this about your sister?"

"Georgiana grew sick in the same way your sister Jane did after the situation at Ramsgate. She had told me in happiness and had not supposed I would be so vehemently against their union. It seems nearly impossible for me to consider what she could have been thinking. I can only believe that her rationale was damaged so severely that she was incapable of proper thought."

"Did she attempt to take her life?"

"Not as such." Sadness filled Darcy's heart as he considered the painful loneliness Georgiana must have experienced. "I wrote to Wickham, and he immediately left the area. She was heartbroken that he did not even try to persuade me. After we returned to London, she grew morose, as I said. One day, I came to her chamber unexpectedly and found her cutting herself. I could scarcely believe it, but she had scars up and down her legs where she had been injuring herself for years."

"But you got her help," Elizabeth said in a sad voice which made Darcy realise she was comparing his actions with those of her parents.

"I hardly knew where to begin. I sought our rector, and he suggested religious training. I found physicians and more clergymen. One of them recommended a woman named Mrs. Annesley, who had once worked in a hospital for the mad. Her husband had been a vicar. She combined her understanding of treating the ill with her faith.

"All the others had told Georgiana that she was lazy or faithless. They prescribed medications and stern treatment. I was not to coddle her. I must be harsh and blame her, let her know her errors, the potential shame she could bring to the family. She rarely spoke, but unless it was apologetic, I should not indulge it. Instead, Mrs. Annesley suggested allowing Georgiana time and space. We should be supportive and let her come to us when she was ready. After a few weeks, she seemed to improve, but Mrs. Annesley told me it would not last. She did well while I was at Netherfield. When I returned to London, she appeared much improved. After a period of forced cheerfulness and what looked like a return to her usual self, we found Georgiana bleeding and curled up in a ball in her closet."

Darcy took a deep breath, aware of Elizabeth now stroking his back as he had done for her. "When she recovered from that episode, she finally broke down and talked about the abuse. She did not see what was wrong with eloping with Wickham when they loved each other. She was certain he loved her because of the intimacies he had taken. Intimacies which she thought were perfectly natural since she had been taught them so young. She had been taught correct principles from others, but they came too late and had only confused her."

A shudder racked through Darcy's frame as he considered the next part. They were coming to the betrayal which stung the most. "My hatred for high society comes from this situation. I approached my uncle, an earl, who knew the man very well. I asked what we could do. The man is also a peer, and I knew suits against them do not fare well. I was uncertain if there had ever been such an allegation heard in court before. I also did not wish for Georgiana to have to testify or for her name to be brought up at all. My uncle at first refused to believe Georgiana's claim. After speaking with her, he accepted her story but said we should do nothing. He said these things happened and they were unfortunate, but it would be much worse to discuss them. He went so far as to say that if I sought justice or spoke of it to anyone else, he would deny it all and cast aspersions upon her and me. Disgusted with London, I sent Georgiana to Pemberley, but I had to remain for several weeks."

Elizabeth shook her head. "I would say I cannot believe family would treat you in such a way, but I, too, know that pain. I am proud of you, though. When denied the opportunity to seek legal redress, others would find the man and give their own justice by the sword or a gun. However, I do not think that sort of revenge gives the peace one desires. It would create a scandal, and you could even be hanged for it. You have been exceedingly strong, sensible, and honourable when others would not be." She pressed a kiss where her head lay over his heart.

Darcy could hardly see the merit of her words. He did not feel as though he had done anything heroic. He simply loved his sister and would not give up on her, just as he would not give up on Elizabeth. That is what one did when they loved. Exhausted, they spoke no more, and Darcy fell into a restful sleep for the first time in months.

Elizabeth awoke with her back pressed against Darcy's chest. His sore arm was wrapped around her waist, and his breath tickled the back of her neck. She had lain awake for a considerable time the night before as she thought about all Darcy had said. She had been so sheltered before leaving Longbourn. She knew leaving was the right decision, and yet she had supposed it was the harshest life a gentlewoman could ever have. She had heard whisperings of very young prostitutes but never thought it could happen to a girl like her.

One time while visiting the Gardiners when she was fourteen, she saw an excessively pretty girl who could not be much older than she was standing outside a tavern. A man approached her and put a coin in her hand before they walked around the alley and out of view. Elizabeth had seen such things in passing many times. It was a fact of living in London and not in the Mayfair district. Gracechurch Street was not a dangerous area, but you could buy all manner of things in

Cheapside and the flesh was one of the bestselling commodities. Prostitutes were often run off. Shopkeepers in the district did not want them offending families or well-to-do ladies, but Mrs. Gardiner had explained it would be worth the risk if they had even one client who paid more. Elizabeth recalled the scene only because of the girl's youth. She had very few of the womanly looks about her. For years, Elizabeth held it in her mind as an acknowledgment that at least her life was better than that girl's. She had never considered that such things could have happened to her sisters or neighbours, under the noses of their parents and guardians.

Elizabeth also had not thought such deviants wore gentlemen's clothes. After her disillusionment with Wickham, she acknowledged he had been merely pretending to be a gentleman. His father had been a solicitor and then a steward. Despite Wickham's words that his father had been devoted to Darcy's, she supposed the elder Wickham would not have become his steward if he were not offered more money. What existence did he have before if becoming a servant—albeit a high and independent one—made more money than being a solicitor? She supposed it must have been like all the poor country curates. It was far easier to be educated at university and seek employment than it was to find a position.

Having the highest opinion, previously, of her uncle Gardiner and many of his merchant friends, Elizabeth did not presume that good values were only found among the gentry. However, her other uncle was often given to over-indulgence of port and was as crude and vulgar as his wife. By contrast, she had never seen such displays from her Bennet relations. She had to admit to herself that the gentry were more polished. She had fooled herself into believing it meant there could be no ugliness in that world.

Poor Miss Darcy! Elizabeth could not conceive going through the suffering that the wealthy young miss had. To be used by George Wickham as part of his dispute with her brother and for her inheritance did not surprise Elizabeth. She had never considered it before, but the wealthy had their trials. A few weeks ago, she might have meanly even thought that it was fair compensation for all they could enjoy with their riches. However, to be attacked by a family friend...

Elizabeth knew she had never been assaulted, but what of her sisters? Jane was always uncommonly beautiful. Did she hide a secret such as Miss Darcy which caused Mr. Bingley's defection to spiral her into grief? She could think of no one who visited as often as it sounded like Mr. Darcy's friend did. Mr. Bennet did not have many friends. He was a private man and disliked Society.

Alternately, Jane did visit the Gardiners in London. Elizabeth hesitated to consider if her uncle were capable of such things, but then she acknowledged the point must be that it was well-hidden. However, in Miss Darcy's situation, the man had befriended her to the exclusion of others. Elizabeth could not recall that ever being the case with Mr. Gardiner or anyone else Jane had ever known.

Mentally shaking her head, she resolved that Jane's melancholy must have derived entirely from Bingley. Elizabeth's mind jumped from Bingley to his sisters. Did the false friends understand the cost of their actions? They made Jane their plaything. Miss Bingley and Mrs. Hurst had promoted a friendship with Jane and then abandoned her when they returned to London. Everyone had taken their willingness to befriend Jane as proof of Mr. Bingley's growing attachment to her. Mrs. Bennet had declared that Jane would soon be the mistress of Netherfield, and only stopped short of ordering wedding clothes by Jane's pleading and her husband's adamant declaration that he would not pay the bill. Elizabeth had laughed at the folly of it all at the time.

She had laughed at so much. She had always chosen to laugh rather than cry. There was no shortage of heartache or grief in the world. Instead, she latched on to the fleeting moments of joy she could find. Her desire to find mirth made her excuse the behaviour of her family. She had told herself, sometimes a thousand times a day, that they meant no harm—indeed, they were harmless. Mr. Bennet's teasing criticism of his wife held no evil. When it descended to his daughters, well, it was just his way of showing affection. Her mother's anxious wailings about their future were nothing but a conscious bid for attention and distinction. With five daughters about, there was always one who could soothe her. Sharp words from her mother to Elizabeth were always well-deserved or due to the matron's silly and ill-formed mind. Elizabeth only saw the rough edges of her family due to her proximity. Surely all others saw them only in a good light. However, if they did not, it did not bear worrying about. Elizabeth did not care for the opinion of strangers.

Then Mr. Bingley and Mr. Darcy arrived in Hertfordshire and turned everything on its head. How she had hated Mr. Darcy! Even more, Elizabeth hated how she cared for his opinion. His rejection at the ball stung. His continued disapproval of the Bennets and Meryton bothered her far more than she wanted to admit at the time. After Lydia and Kitty eloped, Elizabeth recognised that she had known it was all well-deserved censure. Now she considered that during all this time the wonderful man holding her had been through hellish trials she could barely conceive.

Even now, she felt the proof of his ardent desire against her. She suspected he was awake, but he made no move to seduce her or take advantage of his state. Elizabeth had suggested they share the bed, and while they slept, their bodies had found each other. In the days since they met again, she grew to understand the strength and comfort one could draw from the embrace of another.

Darcy loved her so much! Her heart fluttered at the thought. If she could turn back time and be the Elizabeth Bennet he had known in Hertfordshire, she was sure she would be in love with him by now. Darcy was the most honourable man she had ever met. It was not a façade he wore only when times were easy. He did not placate or charm but instead was honest and frank. He was reserved, it was true, but that was no crime. There was a time when being of good character and loving her was all she had ever wanted in a spouse. It was all it would have taken to win her heart. Maybe someday it would be again.

Elizabeth stroked the hand that rested on her waist.

"Good morning, my love," he whispered into her neck.

A shiver ran down Elizabeth's spine, and goose pimples erupted over her flesh. She was beginning to love how he could affect her. "Did you sleep well?" she asked.

"I have not rested so well in months. Thank you for listening and for your understanding last night." He nuzzled his face into the space between her neck and shoulder. "Your skin is so soft," he murmured as he kissed her exposed flesh.

The hand around Elizabeth's waist tightened. His palm stretched almost entirely from under her breast to her hip. The single motion of reflexively clenching his fist, resulting in a moderate increase in pressure as his digits ran over her covered skin, combined with his growing ardour was the headiest sensation she had ever felt. He ran a finger in lazy circles over her side, making her dizzy as she arched her neck to give him further access to explore.

She felt him inhale deeply and hold it before releasing his breath. She imagined that he ached in longing just as she did.

"We should rise for the day," he declared before releasing her and sitting up.

Elizabeth had never hated the idea of awakening more.

Chapter Nine

Throughout the day, Elizabeth paused now and then in reading or listening to Darcy to observe him. More than once, he caught her staring, causing her to blush—something he seemed to enjoy profusely. She did not know that she could truly love him—certainly not as he deserved. However, she admired him more than ever. As a young lady of twenty, she had been infatuated with several men before. Indeed, she had even been infatuated with Wickham. It quickly faded to indifference and friendship before souring entirely. In the months apart from Darcy, she had come to see him as the best of men just because he was the opposite of Wickham in every way. Now, she knew the real strength of his character. He bore what no other man ever could!

What had she done when life grew too unbearable? She had run away and left her sisters behind. Even now, the guilt tore at her. She tortured herself late at night when Darcy was asleep with thoughts of how she might have made her parents see reason. She might have found help for Jane, just as Darcy had for his sister. Some rational part of her would argue back the impossibilities of it all. Darcy was a man and wealthy. He was his sister's guardian. He had many freedoms that Elizabeth and her sisters did not have.

The thoughts did not expunge her feelings of guilt, however, for she could not forgive herself for all the years of ignoring and absolving her parents' grievous errors. How often had Mrs. Bennet cooed about the outstanding match beautiful Jane would eventually make? Each year a deeper note of disappointment had entered Mrs. Bennet's voice as Jane remained unwed. However, she always remained adamant that soon Jane would marry well, and they would have no reason to fear Mr. Bennet's demise. As her father never seemed to take the possibility of his death seriously, Elizabeth merely rolled her eyes at her mother's lamenting. They had kind and loving relatives. Mr. Bennet had some money set aside for his wife and daughters per the marriage articles.

It was apparent to Elizabeth that what Mrs. Bennet would most miss was the ability to be mistress of Longbourn. She feared any loss of position. The mother of a well-established daughter was not as insignificant as a widow with five spinster daughters. However, the fears were real to Mrs. Bennet and infected every aspect of her life. Family meals at Longbourn were always satisfactory but nothing special. However, if a single gentleman was invited, it had to be a lavish affair.

Elizabeth wondered how much of her father's income was spent on entertaining possible suitors. They needed new clothing every year regardless of whether it was truly necessary. There were constant trips to the milliner for the latest accessories. Seeing it now through distant eyes, Elizabeth realised there was some aspect of Mrs. Bennet that did not want to appear the wretched and pitiable woman even before her husband's demise. The more sensible it might have been to economise—as more and more daughters reached a marriageable age and yet the eldest remained unwed, and therefore it was likely that one or more of them might never marry—the more frenzied Mrs. Bennet became in her shopping. She grew calculating and devious in her desire to ensnare husbands for her daughters. She never once considered that the daughters she sought to protect felt perfectly content at home.

Elizabeth considered what it must have looked like to Kitty and Lydia. To them, it must have seemed that they might never marry. They would never have a moment to shine with Elizabeth and Jane still at home and Mrs. Bennet doggedly pursuing husbands for them. The incident with Mr. Collins was a prime example. He could not have Jane, for in Mrs. Bennet's eyes she was as good as engaged to Mr. Bingley. Elizabeth was offered as a substitute without any thought about her own desires or if she would suit as a parson's wife. It would have been much better to suggest Mary, but no, Mrs. Bennet could not give her attention, and her youngest daughters were meant for greater things. Even as Kitty and Lydia were spared the consideration of Mr. Collins, they must have seen that they would have had little choice in selecting their own suitor when their time came. Instead, they took matters into their own hands.

Elizabeth had spent years telling herself that her family's errors were harmless or even lovable. She was overly critical of them, but no one else seemed to notice. They were not shunned in Meryton or the surrounding area. Elizabeth now admitted to herself that there were always flaws in that way of thinking. Why was Jane still unmarried? No gentleman had even proposed to her!

Meanwhile, Elizabeth attracted the attention of men she could never consider. She did not doubt that if it were not for the chance encounter with Darcy at the inn, she never would have seen him again. He loved her, but he would have been willing to live without her all his life. That did not mean she doubted his love; she merely acknowledged that life was not fair. She had liked Wickham very much, but his insufficient income was too great an obstacle for a sensible woman like herself. She could never marry a man she did not respect, such as Mr. Collins. Elizabeth had none of Jane's reserve, and while not as beautiful, she was very pretty. Surely men sometimes married vivacious and pretty girls with silly families and little money.

If Elizabeth's pitiful dowry was such a hindrance, then certainly her parents would have added to it. Perhaps it would not have appealed to most of the gentlemen of their acquaintance, but it might supplement a merchant's income well enough. Why were they not brought more into that circle? Their uncle Gardiner would have been an excellent source of acquaintances from that sphere. While Jane and Elizabeth often visited the Gardiners, they seldom entered Society, and the Gardiners entertained even less frequently. It was as if no one seriously thought about how to launch the girls into Society. Or, when she was feeling particularly uncharitable, it was as though they simply did not care or even wished them ill.

The sadder but more realistic explanation was that they were too self-absorbed to consider it. Elizabeth winced as she heard her mother's voice echo in her ears. Everything her daughters did was an extension of herself. She boasted of Jane's beauty, and in the next breath explained that she had been considered the most handsome girl in the county in her youth. Lydia's good-naturedness was only surpassed by her own. Even Mary's dogged persistence at the pianoforte and obliviousness to the pleasure of her audience matched Mrs. Bennet's drive to marry a gentleman and her lack of self-knowledge when others tired of her antics.

Elizabeth was always viewed as suspicious by Mrs. Bennet. In her second daughter, she could see nothing like herself. Elizabeth was too quick-witted, too sharp-mouthed, and too irreverent. She had beauty and liveliness but did not put them to use in the way Mrs. Bennet would have or in a way that she could put herself to the best advantage. As such, Mrs. Bennet was forever scolding Elizabeth. In the same way that her other daughters' triumphs were her own, Elizabeth's failures were a reflection of her own.

As much as Elizabeth could acknowledge all of this and know the falsehood it presented, she could not turn off the voice in her head that she had heard since birth. Although she never valued her mother or respected her opinions, she had somehow mentally adopted her words, and they were now how she talked about herself. As wrong as she knew it was, Elizabeth was helpless against the criticisms in her head. They intruded in moments of quiet, such as now, and she felt like a prisoner in her own mind.

If she truly had been better than her mother and not as self-absorbed, then she would have noticed Jane's growing melancholy. She would have noticed Mary's increasing dependence on alcohol. She would have seen the frenzied desire Lydia had to leave Longbourn. If she were as clever as she had always considered herself to be, then she would have foreseen Miss Bingley's treatment of Jane. She could have cautioned her sister not to depend so much upon the possibility in that quarter. Instead, at every moment, she assured her sister of Mr. Bingley's love—long after Jane doubted it herself. What damage she had wreaked!

Fidgeting in her seat, Elizabeth felt Darcy's eyes upon her. She looked up.

"You are restless again," he said.

Elizabeth merely shrugged. There was nothing either one of them could do about it at the moment. She was attempting to stay in good humour while she desperately wished to escape the walls of the room. Now, filled with thoughts of her family and her own errors, it felt stifling—suffocating even.

"I have a deck of cards. We could play something."

"If you wish," she said.

Inwardly, she cringed. She had done it again. Was she subconsciously becoming her mother? Surely Mrs. Bennet had concealed much about herself to ensnare Mr. Bennet. Elizabeth was aware of her circumstances. She truly admired Mr. Darcy, and he was a human saviour to her. She should be wise not to ruin his perceptions.

As Darcy located his cards, she scolded herself. Was she too much like Mrs. Bennet, or was she concealing because she always did the wrong thing? Either way, her response to him was wrong.

"What are you thinking about?" Darcy asked when he returned to his seat.

Reaching for something to say lest he know her frenzied and confused thoughts, she answered with a deceitfully calm smile. "I just realised that I never inquired after our mutual acquaintances. How are Mr. Bingley and his sisters? I suppose you might see them often."

"No, I do not see them very often," Darcy said as he dealt. "I was not in London for very long before going on to Pemberley. After learning about truth of Georgiana's abuse, we journeyed to the estate. I returned to Town only for business reasons and once she had seemed to improve."

"Miss Bingley was correct, then, when she had written to Jane and told her that you were anxious to see your sister?"

"Indeed. Although she could hardly know why. It certainly added to my reasons for wishing to be away from Hertfordshire in such a hurry. Mrs. Annesley's letters indicated that Georgiana might relapse."

Elizabeth tilted her head just as Darcy's hand slowed, as though he realised he had said something he did not intend. "Your anxieties over her *added* to your reasons? Why else did you desire to leave?"

Darcy continued to lay out cards and avoided meeting Elizabeth's eyes. She narrowed hers before touching one of his hands to cease his movements. "Fitzwilliam?"

Finally, he lifted his head and took in her expression. Elizabeth hoped to disarm him with an inviting smile. He frowned, apparently unimpressed. The man truly had spent too much time observing her in Hertfordshire if he knew when she was faking calm.

"I owe you the truth. It should come as no surprise given the other matters we have discussed. I felt too attracted to you and believed separation would be the best way to sever the bonds. I had argued as much to Bingley."

"To Bingley?"

"He was determined to return to Netherfield, and I admit that I persuaded him to remain in London."

"You!" Elizabeth could say nothing more as the room began to spin. She had fixed in her mind that it was all the work of Bingley's sister. What could Mr. Darcy object to if his own family was as flawed as hers?

The thought of betrayal from yet another source she had come to rely upon filled her with a need to bolt. However, never before had she felt so dizzy, so incapable of moving, and so close to sickness. Her throat clenched, blocking all sound and nearly choking her. She attempted to breathe but could not get enough air. Her last conscious thought was that she would rather rant and scream than faint.

When Elizabeth awoke, she was in bed, and the surgeon from a few days before waved something foul-smelling beneath her nose. "Please, no," she said.

"You see," the doctor turned to Darcy, "there was no reason to fear. I think I know what would cause her to faint." He looked back at Elizabeth. "Would you like him to leave? It is not customary that men are present for the examination."

"Pardon me? I do not need an examination."

"You could wait for the midwife once you reach your destination, but the earlier you begin care, the better."

"Midwife!" Elizabeth screeched. "Excuse me, sir, but there is absolutely no need for a midwife. I guarantee it."

The man turned to look at Darcy, who vigorously nodded. "If you and your husband are certain—"

"He is not my husband."

"Pardon me. I had thought that given the arrangement...but it is none of my business."

"Miss Bennet is my betrothed. We are on our way to be wed," Darcy explained.

"Oh," the surgeon said in understanding. "And you are certain there would be no need..."

"Absolutely not," Elizabeth said and glared at Darcy. She thought his valet had clarified matters. "I had a shock, that is all. Thank you for your time and care."

Effectively dismissed and apparently understanding that an angry female was not trouble he wished to borrow, the surgeon packed up quickly. After he left, Darcy hastened to Elizabeth's side.

"Are you truly well? I have seldom been more terrified. You turned as white as snow!"

"I am confident you were more concerned when your sister, the great Miss Darcy with lofty connections and a large fortune, lay bleeding in her chamber from a self-inflicted wound."

Darcy sucked in a deep breath. "I have angered you—wounded you somehow. I know you would never say such a thing if you were not so upset."

Immediately, remorse seared Elizabeth's heart. She was hurting, desperately so. She had thought she was entirely incorrect in her first understanding of Darcy. However, now it seemed only too correct. He was too proud to like the Bennets or Meryton. He had poisoned Bingley against Jane. Jane, the dearest, sweetest girl who ever lived and her closest friend and confidant. The same Jane who became so depressed at Bingley's abandonment that she wanted to take her own life. The Jane she had abandoned. All the guilt and despair that had tormented Elizabeth for weeks now laid on Darcy's shoulders. Yes, she would cling to that anger! Miss Darcy might not have deserved Elizabeth's censure, but her brother surely did.

She looked at him anew. Had she thought she loved him a few moments ago? She could never love a man who had been so careless in his actions that led to such awful misery. He was just like them. He proved to be just like every other selfish person she had valued. Her mother, father, aunt, uncle—they all turned their backs on her and held onto vain pretensions. If they only erected a false image to the world on the outside, then all would be well on the inside. Meanwhile, even now, Jane might lie dead beneath the ground.

"Let go of me," Elizabeth hissed as she attempted to pull her hand out from under his.

He obeyed with apparent regret and settled his hands on his knees as he sat in the chair next to her bed.

"And go over there!" She pointed at the settee.

"Can we not talk about it? I do not know why my information upset you so."

Fire exploded in Elizabeth's eyes. "You should know what you did to upset me. If you cannot think of that, then I want nothing to do with you."

"Surely you do not mean that. I cannot know your mind."

Elizabeth raised her brows and glared. After a moment, she lifted her chin and turned her face. She would not even look at him. Eventually, she heard him shuffle away.

As soon as she could walk, Elizabeth mentally vowed, she would leave the inn and Darcy. She would start over. She had done it once before, and she could do it again. This time, she would know not to rely on anyone but herself. Fairy tales were only things told to children. Mr. Darcy was the cruellest man to ever exist.

Chapter Ten

Elizabeth's anger mellowed to a simmer by the time darkness fell. She had still not spoken to Darcy again, despite a few attempts on his side. If her ankle had permitted it, she would have left hours ago. However, as she was bound to the bed with not even a book to read—that would have required asking Darcy for assistance—she had nothing but her thoughts.

When she had left Longbourn, it was because there was no other way. Indeed, she had not intended to leave it forever or leave her sisters permanently behind. Her aunt and uncle had chosen to betray her rather than help. Elizabeth thought she learned her lesson on trusting others. Yet here she was, entirely dependent upon Darcy. He had rescued her as much as any knight in shining armour had a damsel in distress. She had not been locked in a tower and there was no fire-breathing dragon, but she was trapped just the same. Fleetingly, Elizabeth wondered if the other damsels feared to let go of their past and all they had known—even if it was imprisonment with fear of death—rather than face an unknown life and trust a stranger.

It was not the unknown which made Elizabeth so uncomfortable. She had faced that before. For her own sake, she could choose it again. However, she had come to rely upon Darcy. She thought him incapable of disappointing her or of showing that selfishness which had invaded every aspect of her life.

Attached to the fact that she had not learned her lesson regarding trusting others, Elizabeth knew she had acted too rashly. Since leaving Longbourn, it seemed as though every decision required an answer that very instant. More than once she had to decipher if a man meant to harm her or if a hallway was safe to enter. The work in the bar itself required fast thinking and hearing orders amidst the loud noise. She needed to be mindful of Cuthbert's demands and attuned to the moods of the other maids. She quickly learned that it did not do to earn the patronage of too many tables lest the other ladies have none. In such an atmosphere, it was better to focus on cooperative work and keep her head down. Perhaps that is when she began agreeing with everything anyone said. The very decision to come to this town and this inn was decided upon the spur of the moment. Elizabeth had prided herself that it would be all the better, then. The Gardiners and Bennets could hardly guess in which direction she fled, and they did not have the resources to search everywhere indefinitely.

The evening wore on, and eventually Darcy excused himself. Molly entered, and seemingly perceiving Elizabeth's mood, did not chatter as usual. By the time Darcy returned, Elizabeth was in bed, feigning sleep. He murmured a good night and laid on the settee.

Rest did not find her that night. Judging by how long it took her to hear Darcy's deep breathing and eventual snores, it took a long time to find him as well. Elizabeth wrestled with her thoughts until just before dawn. Instinctively, she knew all of this went far deeper than anything Darcy had said or done.

The Elizabeth who trusted Wickham had trusted too easily. Since Darcy left Hertfordshire, there had been blow after blow in Elizabeth's life, all teaching her not to think well of others. Everyone had their own motive, and it had nothing to do with her well-being. If she did not wish to be trampled by life, she should take care of herself first. Indeed, she was powerless to do anything else. If she could not save Jane, she could not save anyone. The piece of old Elizabeth who could see the good in people and make some allowance for their character—the part that had been influenced by Jane, Elizabeth mused— whispered to allow Darcy time to explain his actions. The new Elizabeth screamed loudly in her mind. She should not trust Darcy or anyone else. Their actions always proved them unreliable.

When at last she fell asleep, she dreamed of two versions of herself on a battlefield. Instead of fighting with guns, they grasped opposite ends of a rope and tugged with all their might. She recognised the Elizabeth of her present thoughts: She wore dirty, ragged clothes. Soot was smeared on her face, and she wore a mean expression. The other Elizabeth looked as though she had no real care in the world. Her gown was soft and spotless. Her countenance held no regrets, only smiles and laughter. Throughout the night, they battled, and when Elizabeth awoke more exhausted than if she had not slept, there was no definite winner.

The dream faded in the stark reality. She was cold and alone in the big bed of the chamber. Hating that she had grown accustomed to waking in Darcy's arms, she mentally scolded herself. Glancing around, she did not see him. Fear replaced the irritation. Where had he gone? Had he left her?

"Why should I care?" Elizabeth asked in frustration as she buried her head in her hands. No tears came, but her head ached and her mind was exhausted from warring with itself.

Darcy knocked and asked if he could enter, his voice immediately calming her. She timidly answered. He entered bearing a tray of tea and breakfast things, taking in her expression.

"I thought you might want to eat. You did not yesterday."

Elizabeth's stomach loudly rumbled in agreement. She had been too angry to think of food. Should she take his offering? Her stomach growled again, her body telling her she was a fool even if her mind would not. Did she think she was independent and could survive without him? He was gone a matter of minutes, and she worried he had left her forever. She could not even acquire food without his assistance!

Determined to at least rectify that, she tossed her legs over the bed and tested the strength of her ankle. Darcy was tinkering with the tea things, and she was halfway to him when he looked up.

"Elizabeth! I would have helped you!" He began to move to her side.

"No. It is gaining strength. It can never heal if I do not test it." As Elizabeth said the words, she realised she might be speaking about more than the swollen joint.

She reached the settee and practically leapt into it, sighing when her weight was off her feet. It had been painful and challenging, but she had done it, and with more practice, it would grow easier. Darcy handed her a teacup, and their fingers grazed. Instead of the usual shock and tingles, she felt relief and comfort at his touch. He was still here, despite her behaviour and actions.

"I apologise for my words about your sister. You were correct; I was very hurt and not thinking clearly. I should allow you to explain."

Darcy ceased stirring his tea and met her eyes. "I am exceedingly sorry to have wounded you. I would be happy to explain, but I do not understand what great sin I committed."

Elizabeth bristled. She was doing more than meeting him halfway. She apologised first, and he still acted as though he were blameless! There was the pride and conceit he hid from her for the last few days. He acted as though it were all a matter of opinion or perspective. She was sure if someone had treated his sister as he had done to Jane, he would feel just as angry.

"Perhaps I ought to have concealed matters," he said. "I should not have told you the truth. However, I do not think our relationship should be based on lies. I knew you would be unhappy for me to voice it, but I thought you understood. You had asked how I could marry you with a damaged reputation, and I said I no longer cared what the *ton* thought. Two nights ago, I explained my reasoning for such. Although I did not outright state it, I had cared what they thought. Their perceptions of me and what they held as right affected me greatly. I chose to leave Hertfordshire rather than fall in love with you. It was only after I left that I realised I had already fallen. I was in the middle before I knew I had begun."

Elizabeth's teacup remained halfway to her mouth during his speech. He thought she was angry on her own behalf? She had accepted that his love was inadequate to the obstacles her situation presented: relations in trade and little dowry. These realities barely troubled her. Could he be so senseless to the wound he had given Jane? Had he not just the other night blamed himself for Lydia? Lowering her cup, she said, "I am not angry for myself. You confessed to convincing Bingley to remain in London."

"The word convince might be a stretch," Darcy said as he leaned back, seemingly accepting that this could be a lengthy discussion. "I said nothing to him that I did not say to myself. I have no special tactics or abilities to control one's mind. For that, you would need to speak with my cousin, the colonel. He oversees querying captive soldiers for information."

"What were these reasons? It did not seem to disturb Mr. Bingley before you spoke with him that we had relations in trade or little money."

Darcy gave her a confused look. "I will admit those would have been greater evils to me than to my friend, but they were not what I discussed. You have explained your reasons for leaving Longbourn to me and have made it seem as though it was all because of a few poor decisions since November. However, you are no fool. You know it goes deeper. I would wager those are the thoughts that torment you when you think I am not looking. Will you hold me accountable for perceiving what you did not until recently?"

Air left Elizabeth's lungs on a whoosh. Had she attempted to blame him when she really blamed herself? Yes. Yes, she certainly had. She ducked her head. "You left Hertfordshire because of my family's behaviour?"

"It was a confluence of things. There was almost a total want of propriety from your mother, three younger sisters, and even your father. It was not one or two actions or statements. It was apparent to me that the Bennet family had many disorderly attributes, and I had no hope of them improving. If they acted that way in public, what happened in private? What evil would befall their minds and work their way into a marriage?"

"And my sisters' elopements are a testament to that!"

"Do not forget that my sister also desired to elope. I did judge harshly when I had no right. My sister hid her misery whereas yours did not. However, Georgiana also chose to tell me about the elopement. She eventually confided in me about her abuse. However, we have left the topic at hand." He sighed. "The evening of the ball at Netherfield, Sir William Lucas made it sound as though the entire area expected a proposal from Bingley—or that he already had, and they only needed to settle a date. I had often seen Bingley in love and had not previously thought anything of his attachment to your sister Jane. After Sir William's words, however, I took careful notice of them. Bingley did display a greater preference than I had ever seen before. Your sister, however, did not. For a lady who could be so assured of Bingley's sentiments—I would say far more assured than most ladies—she seemed to take no pleasure in his attention or the inevitable outcome. Your mother loudly crowed all evening of her intended goals for Jane—and all of you. It would not be unusual for a docile daughter to follow her mother's choices. If my own observation of Jane had not been enough, your mother constantly declared Jane the most biddable and agreeable daughter. I believed it probable she would marry where directed without regard to her own feelings. A marriage built upon that would be nothing but disaster. Bingley would be in love, and Jane was not and might never be."

"Do you not see you have struck the very bargain you had hoped to keep your friend from?"

"Yes! To him, I have been kinder than to myself!"

Elizabeth marvelled that he could congratulate himself on sparing his friend's feelings until she took in his countenance. Dark circles had appeared under his eyes since their argument the previous evening. The acknowledgment that she might never love him had torn at him. The anguish he had when explaining about Miss Darcy was once again evident on his face. "You did not think Jane might have learned to love him?"

"To me, it appeared that was unlikely or that she would even have the opportunity with your mother rushing them to the altar. I have seen marriages like that. They end up despising one another as neither can give what the other most wants. We cannot be other people. We can only be ourselves, no matter how much we might try otherwise."

Was that for her? Elizabeth's conscience niggled at her, even though she would have rather thought it applied to him as his pride had re-emerged after all. Oh, he had been so arrogant and conceited to think he could decipher Jane's feelings from his limited observation. However, one thing was clear: It was done in compassion. He intended to save his friend from the feelings now tormenting him.

"I cannot explain it any better than that, Elizabeth," he said. "I am a human, and I made an error. However, young couples in love are often separated, and they do not resort to what Jane did. You cannot make me responsible for her feelings any more than you are responsible for them."

Incapable of forming words immediately after such blows, Elizabeth remained silent. Instead of replying, she chose to finish her tea and read for several hours—or rather to hold a book, as the pages could not interest her.

She had thought Darcy incapable of disappointing her. Then she felt because he had that he must have been as motivated by selfishness as her relations. She had despaired of every good thing about him. The guilt of such thoughts weighed heavily upon her, for had she not seen his kind heart and actions over the last several days?

The ability to err and it not be a grievous wrong, that it was not with the intention to hurt or acknowledged later with an apology, was foreign to her. It was freeing, too. For weeks she had wondered if she had done wrong by leaving Jane and Mary at Longbourn. It was not done with that intention, but that is where the decision led. Now, she acknowledged to herself, there were things outside her control. She never could direct their feelings or how they handled a crisis. Why did Jane become so melancholy over Bingley? Whether or not it was a mistake to leave Longbourn, there could be recovery. She only needed to forgive herself.

"I have been thinking," he said after an hour or two of silence. "If you believe your ankle is healed enough to travel, you could start on the journey tomorrow. It might be better if we do not travel together. You might enjoy the privacy and freedom to keep your own hours."

"You wish me to leave you?" Elizabeth asked as sorrow filled her heart.

"No." Darcy sighed. "The close confines have not served us well, I think. The sleeping arrangement is not what it should be, and I feel as though I am forcing you into things you do not prefer."

Elizabeth returned her attention to her book, forcing herself to think for several minutes before replying. While Darcy spoke earlier, she had the realisation that she no longer wished to be carried by her emotions. She had reasoned that before, but as she did not understand why she had come to rely upon them, she could not end the habit. Finally, she set her book aside. "I have been thinking about everything all wrong. I had thought you rescued me, which rankled my pride even as I welcomed the reprieve. However, I think we are saving each other and learning to work together as a proper marriage requires. I must see things from your perspective, and you must see some of mine."

"I am very willing to listen," he encouraged.

"I apologise for blaming you for Jane's feelings. I can see how it appeared to you and that you meant no harm. Indeed, the harm that did befall was unlikely. Additionally, I suppose you are correct. There must be some deeper problems at work for her to feel as she did. I am beginning to recognise there are for me, too. Despite Jane's goodness, she could not be immune to the devastation our parents wreaked."

Elizabeth paused to see if Darcy still listened. He met her eyes and seemed to smile encouragingly. Elizabeth explained to him all she had recently realised. It was nothing compared to the trials his sister faced and it did not manifest in the way it had with Jane, but it crippled her all the same.

It was as though she had lived with a disease for many years, and now it finally attempted to make its claim upon her life. Mr. and Mrs. Bennet had never truly been the parents of Longbourn. That role fell to Jane and Elizabeth—mostly the latter, as Jane was too kind-hearted to scold or anticipate deceit and poor decisions. It was not enough to merely acknowledge that Mr. and Mrs. Bennet were responsible for the actions of their daughters. Elizabeth was the one who had tried to manage everything and everyone. She had believed she did a better job of it than either parent, and yet her family disintegrated around her.

Somewhere in the middle of the exhausting retelling, Darcy had come to her side. He wrapped his arms around her, lending her strength and comfort. Elizabeth melted into his side.

"I fear it may take years to unlearn all the broken thinking with which I was raised."

"That is perfectly acceptable," Darcy said. "You are not alone in that. We all learn things from our parents and must choose to improve as adults."

"I like how you say that. I choose to improve, although it is not easy, and I am terrified."

"You do not have to do it alone," he murmured against her ear. "Have you decided if you would prefer to journey ahead of me?"

As much as Elizabeth acknowledged that she needed to regain control of her impulses and emotions, she did not hesitate to squeeze Darcy tightly and kiss him before answering. "No. I do not wish to part from you. We will make our way together."

Darcy answered with a searing kiss.

Chapter Eleven

Darcy pulled his wife closer. His wife! How often he had dreamt of calling Elizabeth that. Here she was, finally in his arms. His lips found the curve of her neck, delighting in the shiver he felt wrack her petite frame. As he kissed her smooth skin, he felt goose pimples emerge. He found her earlobe and sucked on it until she let out a breathy exhale. The hand around her waist wandered north. She was so soft, so comforting, so everything he had ever needed but never knew. Her bud tightened under his palm, and her sharp inhale brought his mind to reality.

The glorious dream evaporated, and Darcy wrenched his hand away as he realised he was not embracing Elizabeth, his loving wife, but instead Elizabeth, his skittish betrothed.

She was still beside him, making neither a sound nor a move. Darcy rolled to his back and raised to his elbows. They were no longer touching, but he could feel the heat from her body still. The taste of her skin was on his mouth, and the feel of her imprinted on his hand.

Fighting through the temptation and embarrassment, his honour demanded he speak. "Touch...you...apologise...pardon..."

He squeezed his eyes shut and let out a growl as his tongue could not form coherent words. Elizabeth sat up as well. She placed a hand on his arm, causing him to jump. The last thing he needed at that moment was her touching him. Desire still coursed through his veins and thrummed in every muscle of his body.

"Fitzwilliam?" Elizabeth coaxed, and finally, he turned his face to hers. "There is no need to apologise. Your touch was heavenly." She picked up his hand and held it in hers.

"I had no right. This is precisely why I suggested you should journey ahead."

"Are you ashamed of what you feel?" Elizabeth's voice was just above a whisper.

"Only of the timing. We are not wed, and even then, I vowed I would not demand any husbandly rights. I wish for you to desire me as much as I long for you."

"I think I do," Elizabeth acknowledged, blushing. "Perhaps not as much and certainly not with as much knowledge or for as long, but your touch is not unwelcome."

The noble part of Darcy's mind stuttered to understand her confession. She was not saying she loved him. She esteemed him enough to feel attraction. She trusted him enough to voice it and know that it would not mark her as wanton. They were engaged to be married and had shared a bed for several nights. Most couples in their position would have gone far past an accidental touch. These were all good signs. However, he was unsure if they were enough to satisfy him.

"What do you feel for me, Elizabeth?" Darcy asked. "We only met again a few days ago, and yet sometimes it feels as if years have passed. I do not wish to rush you. However, I confess to confusion. Sometimes you seem nearly enamoured of me. You have said you esteem and respect me, but you have also been quick to doubt me. You have attempted to flee more than once."

"Those are my failings, not yours. Trusting you makes me uncomfortable."

Darcy sucked in a breath. He had known it to be true, had he not?

"It is not because of anything you have done or said. My fears and doubts are not a reflection of you or even reality. I am attempting to improve. I have spent my entire life only depending upon myself, but I do trust you. In time, my unease will pass away. I know you shall not give me any reason to doubt or regret you."

It was hardly the stuff of romance. However, Elizabeth had been so wounded that perhaps she did not wish for poetry, flowers, and flattery as most ladies did during courtship.

Interrupting his thoughts, she tugged on him to lie back down. She nestled against him, her head resting over his heart in what had become a favourite position for him. She let out a happy sigh.

"I feel safe here with you, like this."

Darcy tightened his arm around her. His injured arm was nearly healed and could stretch out to add to the embrace. "Does my holding you give you comfort?"

Elizabeth nodded against his chest.

"It brings me comfort as well," he said. "It settles something in my soul—something only you can satisfy. I love you so very much." He pressed a kiss to her hair.

He held her in silence for so long that he thought she had fallen back asleep. It was just as well with him if she preferred to rest in bed all day. Holding her was far preferable to going through the motions of a regular day. They had both tired of reading and sitting in silence in this room. He was just beginning to wonder if they could leave on the morrow when Elizabeth spoke.

"What is love, Fitzwilliam? I do not think I know anymore."

"There are many types of love, of course. I think at its root is a selfless desire for the other's well-being and a feeling of belonging. You accept and acknowledge the other's faults without it lessening their value."

"I do not know that I have ever felt that," Elizabeth whispered. "So much of my life was merely a duty to others."

"I can perfectly understand that. However, did you walk through three miles of mud to take care of Jane at Netherfield only out of duty? She was not gravely ill."

"Who could do less for Jane? No, caring for her was never a duty."

"Then that is one person you have loved. Elizabeth," Darcy said as he pulled her up to meet his eyes, "you have a very great capacity to love. Are you concerned that you do not?"

"I have felt empty and broken for so long." Tears glittered in her eyes.

"You have felt unloved, but I do not believe for one moment that love did not drive all your actions and thoughts."

"Perhaps I was only as selfish as my parents."

"We have already established there was no selfishness in visiting Jane. Indeed, I can think of few places you would have preferred less than to be at Netherfield."

"I did not do enough for my other sisters. I preferred Jane's company because she was the easiest and could soothe me. I shunned Kitty and Lydia, and look at what they did."

"You did not reward their ill-behaviour. Did you view their actions with concern?"

"Certainly."

"And did you think about yourself then?"

"No, I feared for them—for their reputations, if not for their strength of mind."

"Now, let us compare matters. Let us recall the evening of Bingley's ball, as I have already explained it was important in my understanding of your family. One of your sisters played the pianoforte."

"You do not need to remind me." Elizabeth groaned. "I was embarrassed by her putting herself forward so much as to perform a second song when her skills could not support it. I pleaded with my father to intervene."

"Indeed? Did you? If you recall, I sat very near you and could hear everything else said at your area of the table. I heard no application."

"I gave him looks which meant I wished him to stop her."

"Ah, so then you are certainly not accountable for the manner in which he did so."

Elizabeth agreed. "However, I was selfish at the time. I feared what Mary's actions would mean for us. My mother was loudly extolling how Jane would marry Bingley. Kitty and Lydia were outrageously flirtatious. How could I not be embarrassed?"

"Momentary embarrassment does not mean you do not love them. Did you fear it meant others whose opinion you valued would cease to admire you?"

"Of course not. Everyone in Meryton was used to our behaviour, and if Mr. Bingley really loved Jane, then he would never blame her for the actions of her family."

"So you worried, then, for their own account. They ought to have known better and have more pride in their own reputations to behave better."

"I suppose that would be the best way to say it."

"That does not sound very selfish to me."

Elizabeth furrowed her brow. "It does not. However, how is that different from my mother?"

"Do you feel like a lesser person because Lydia eloped?" Elizabeth shook her head. "Has Jane's situation affected your perception of yourself?"

"No. However, I blame myself for the things we spoke of yesterday."

"I do not mean to say that you should blame yourself for those reasons. However, it's certainly not due to selfishness. You have not thought of yourself in all of this."

"When I left Longbourn, I did."

"You left to seek help because you could no longer bear the problems at home. You intended to make matters better for others no matter the cost to yourself. Even now, you speak of Jane and Mary often."

"I was exhausted from it all," Elizabeth whispered. "I felt as fragile as glass and knew I would be the next to break."

"It is not selfish to care for yourself, especially when no one else is capable of doing such." Darcy kissed her forehead. "However, you are no longer alone. I care for you. You need only ask."

Elizabeth let out a deep exhale. "It will take some time to get used to the idea of not blaming myself. I have spent my life being measured to my mother and have always prided myself in not being like her. My greatest fear was that I became her by rashly choosing to leave Longbourn and indulging in what was best for me alone."

"Do not be so harsh on yourself. I think you can agree you have deeply loved your family. You have accepted all their flaws. However, you despise yourself. You demand unreasonable perfection."

Elizabeth blinked rapidly at his words. "I had not considered that before."

He wished he could tell her that he would love her enough for both of them, but he believed that would be insufficient. Even if he could convince her of that, one day she would be angry that she relied entirely on him for feelings of worth. She needed to learn to be satisfied with herself, and he could not do that work for her.

"Speaking of love, I have been wondering if you think I ought to inform Bingley of my error. Would Jane welcome his suit if he returned to Netherfield?"

Elizabeth sighed. "I do not know. I do not know that she is well enough to be courted by anyone. She would hate that I broke her confidence and told you of her feelings at all. I wish there were some way for me to know how she fared."

"Why not write to her?"

"I cannot. I do not wish for my family to discover my location."

"You felt that way when you first arrived because you feared they would take you back to Longbourn. It was one of the first things you said to me. However, no one can forcibly remove you, and I will not allow them. We are betrothed, and I will not give you up." He smiled before raising her hand to his lips.

"I suppose I could try. By the time the letter arrived, we might have already left. I would have to indicate where to send the reply and when we expected to be there. However, there would be no way they could journey there faster than us."

"I doubt they would even try or confront us at all. They would probably only be relieved that you were safe, even if they refused to acknowledge their part in your situation."

"Thank you," Elizabeth said before kissing him. "I can hardly tell you how pleased I am to write to Jane."

"Your kiss spoke for you very well," he said before claiming one for himself.

"Then I shall communicate more in such a wa—"

Darcy's lips landed on hers, ceasing her words.

The sun was high in the sky before they ordered breakfast and Darcy sent for a maid to assist Elizabeth in dressing. They had agreed to leave on the morrow and spend the day in bed with each other. Amidst more light-hearted conversation than they had previously indulged in, they each grew bolder in their caresses. As they learned their bodies and the preferences of both, they discovered a shared affinity for history, poetry, and certain novels. Elizabeth had never been beyond London and delighted in hearing Darcy's descriptions of Pemberley and the adjacent area, as well as his memories of Scotland and Ireland. He fell asleep with a pleased smile on his face. Some things were even better than dreams.

Chapter Twelve

A heavy weight draped across Elizabeth's midsection when she awoke the morning of their departure from the inn. Darcy's palm gently cupped a breast. Although her ankle was still weak, she looked forward to the journey. The quicker they got to Scotland the better, in her opinion.

Beside her, Darcy stirred. He pulled her closer and kissed the exposed skin of her neck. "I love waking up to you in my arms."

Elizabeth grinned and burrowed closer against him. "You always shall, until death do us part."

Before her upset about Bingley and Jane, Elizabeth had thought she was more than halfway to being in love with Darcy. Now she had lost some of her restraint. Why should she not love him? He was deserving of it, and she was willing. He declared she also was worthy of love... That she found more difficult to believe.

Such thoughts evaporated from her mind, however, as Darcy's hand proceeded to wander. His fingers grazed the skin of her collarbone and the tops of her shoulders. Elizabeth sighed at the sensation.

"Do you enjoy it when I touch you like this?"

"Yes." Elizabeth's answer sounded more like a breathy moan, and she arched herself, wordlessly begging him to continue.

"Roll over and face me," Darcy said.

Elizabeth immediately obeyed. For several minutes, Darcy worshipped her lips. Slowly, one hand began to wander over her curves. His hand made lazy circles until, reaching the centre of one breast, he pulled at the tight bud. His hand continued its work as his mouth ceased his ministrations, uttering instead:

"While walking down yonder path one Spring day,

I espied a Summer bud wild and free.

It grew among the weeds and hay

Wind and frost rose up, I could not leave it be.

Pruning, sheltering, and nurturing

It survived and grew full height, you see,

Loudly now the church bells ring,

My wild Summer bloom ne'er fails to delight me,

As it drinks up the sunlight's ray."

As he recited the words, Darcy pulled open the ribbon in front of Elizabeth's nightgown, gently pushing it aside. His eyes never left hers as his hand stroked her skin. The warmth from his palm was welcome on the cool, early Spring day, yet her body shivered with each graze of his flesh against hers.

Darcy alternated pressure during his exploration, sometimes eliciting a gentle sigh, other times a long moan from her lips. Her mind could barely form a coherent thought. "Did you write that?"

"Yes."

"It is beautiful." Elizabeth sighed as his hand continued to work over her body. Perhaps it was not the most laudable piece of poetry compared with the works of the greats, but it sounded infinitely superior to her ears.

"You are beautiful." He nudged more of the fabric over, and his eyes finally left hers, gazing in the exposed skin. "So very beautiful."

"When did you write it?"

"I considered a few lines of it last autumn. More pieces came to me during the winter. However, the final line occurred to me just now."

He pulled back, and Elizabeth smiled as a ray of sunshine bathed her flesh in a yellow glow. "You wrote it about me?"

"Yes." Darcy answered as his eyes followed the circles his fingers made. "You are my wild summer bloom, Elizabeth. And I will care for you through the storms which would destroy you. You think you are the problem, but you have only grown too early and in a difficult position."

Elizabeth sighed as tears pricked her eyes. This was what it felt like to be loved, to be genuinely and unconditionally loved. She pulled Darcy's head to hers and told him all the whispers of her heart in the only way she knew.

Later, they separated to prepare for their journey. Elizabeth decided to return to her old chamber and visit with Molly and any of the other maids who might be there, as it was still early in the day.

"La! She is to leave today." Molly's voice rang out through the open door to the maids' quarters.

Elizabeth stopped outside to hear more.

"You ought to have seen her preening in his room," Molly continued, "as though she were a duchess or married to a prince."

"But how can they be married?" one of the other barmaids asked. "Do you think she left him? I knew a girl once who did. She said she would go back as soon as he could learn to be grateful for what he had."

"They ain't married. She kept saying he would marry her and give her his name, but I don't believe it for one minute. She will be Lizzy Smith forever—if that is even her real name! We know Cordelia uses a false one."

"The men like thinking they are with a fancy piece," the named maid sniffed. "They would much rather have Cordelia in their arms for a tryst than Nellie."

"I thought you were going with them," one of the other maids said to Molly.

"Well, isn't that just like her? You remember when she first came? I said she was too uppity to make friends with the likes of us."

"But she did," someone offered timidly.

"Like she had any choice! But you see how she really treats her friends. Said I couldn't come with them, but I would bet she doesn't want anyone knowing about her past."

Elizabeth pushed open the door. "I thought you just said you doubted he would marry me at all."

The other girls immediately gasped and blushed. A few stammered an apology.

"What do you want, Lizzy? Thought you were leaving to be with your fancy mister," Molly said with a raised chin.

"I wanted to say goodbye to people who I thought were my friends. I can see now I was mistaken. You know I never said you would leave with us. Did you ever count yourself as my friend, or was it only when I had a greater opportunity than you that you became jealous and spiteful, Molly?"

"Don't act like you wouldn't say the same thing to any of us."

"No, I would not."

"Then you are stupider than I thought. Good luck with your man. He will grow tired of you, just like whoever you came from. I would bet your keeper even kicked you out."

Elizabeth stared at the young woman she had called a friend for months. Had Molly always been so mean and she just had not seen it before? Casting her mind back, Elizabeth did see the signs. She had done the same with her family as well. She always made excuses for people.

Elizabeth left the room and found Darcy waiting for her in their chamber. He was ready to depart. The bill was settled with Cuthbert, and the carriage waited for them. Elizabeth hated the uneasiness that was in his eyes. Had she thought she was not returning? Did he think she would argue about hiring Molly?

The start of their journey was quiet, and it took some time for Elizabeth's mood to lighten. Just as quickly as it improved, her good humour evaporated. They were nearing London, and she could not forget her aunt and uncle or the wrong they had done her.

"Will we stay in London for the night?" Elizabeth asked.

"No, I did not think you would prefer it. My valet arranged for us to stay a few hours from here. We will stop in Town only long enough for me to sign the final drafts with my solicitor. Did you post your letter to Jane? If not, we surely can while we are here."

Elizabeth admitted that she had not put it in the post. She had intended to do so after speaking with her friends but entirely forgot after hearing their gossip.

While Darcy spoke with his solicitor, Elizabeth waited in the coach. She watched people from the carriage window and even thought she saw Miss Bingley. She was on the arm of a wealthy looking man and looked as carefree as when Elizabeth last saw her. Had it only been five months? It felt as though it had been years—lifetimes. She thought about how insufficient she had felt compared to Miss Bingley's list of accomplished ladies in November, and how much worse she would be considered now after labouring for her bread. She considered how even girls she had known closely and unguardedly for months thought she had prostituted herself. Molly's last statement stung the most—that Darcy would tire of her.

Leaning back against the squabs, Elizabeth closed her eyes to keep the tears at bay. She focused on breathing in and out while counting to ten in English and French. By the time Darcy returned to the carriage, she had begun to hum an Italian aria she had always liked. Not only did it remind her of the positive things about who she was as Elizabeth Bennet, but it also helped preoccupy her mind. In that vein, she found things to chatter about until they reached their first inn.

Darcy grasped Elizabeth's hand as the carriage came to a stop. "I hate to present it in such a way, but as we will be feigning a marriage, I thought you should wear this." He pulled a simple band from his breast pocket and held it for her inspection.

Elizabeth nodded and removed a hand from her gloves. She knew as much as he did that she had to play a role. Still...something seemed lacking. "Do you think...do you think we could say the words? We could just say our vows now, and although it is not legal, it would mean something when I wore this. It would not be as much of a lie." She had grown ever so tired of lying.

"When we really wed, you will wear a Darcy heirloom ring. Until we reach Scotland, we shall present ourselves as Mr. and Mrs. Smith to be less conspicuous. However, no matter our name or the jewellery on your hand, I will eagerly say our vows and faithfully keep them."

They rushed through their makeshift wedding ceremony, with Elizabeth promising to love and obey Darcy. It was the first time she had said the words, and she hoped more than ever that she could make them true.

"With this ring, I thee wed," Darcy said as he slid the band over her finger, then raised her hand for a kiss. Smiling, he added, "I love you."

Elizabeth wordlessly returned the gesture, although he wore no ring. She knew he loved her. He had orchestrated all of this for her. For now, that would be enough.

That night, as he held her in bed, Elizabeth confessed to her altercation with Molly. She aired the feelings which had nagged her all day.

"Do I not deserve genuine friends? Perhaps if I had been more open—"

"There was nothing about you that could change her. You are very worthy of friendship, and I think once you are in a larger circle of acquaintance you will find some. She provided you with companionship when you most needed it, but she is really just another weed that needs pruning."

"I am sorry if I was in a sour mood. The day started off so well..." Elizabeth sighed with the memories of Darcy's touch.

"I shall happily repeat my actions from this morning," he murmured before capturing her lips.

Chapter Thirteen

D arcy and Elizabeth had sat in companionable silence in the carriage the following day for nearly an hour before she spoke.

"Fitzwilliam, tell me about your friends, your family, the people who make up your life."

Darcy started at her interest. "I have already told you about my sister. You will soon get to know her better. You will meet her companion and nurse, Mrs. Annesley. She is a very genteel lady."

"What about anyone else? You mentioned a cousin who is also Miss Darcy's guardian and relatives that might visit her while you are away. How frequently do you see Mr. Bingley?"

"Richard is often posted to the Continent. When he is not, he is busy with his regiment in London. One day, I hope you two will meet. Aunt Katherine and Uncle Joseph live in Edinburgh, and we do not get to visit with them very often." He frowned a little before answering her final question. "I do not see Bingley more than once or twice a year, although I would say he is my closest friend. He is always getting about—a house party here or there, a soiree in Town, a trip to Scarborough. I much prefer to visit with him at Pemberley."

Elizabeth thought for a moment. "That is just what I would have expected."

"That I hate Society so much that I have only one friend whom I rarely see?"

Elizabeth shook her head as she gathered Darcy's hand and raised it to her lips. "I have discovered you value time together free of other distractions or activities. At the assembly in Meryton, you barely spoke. However, you were talkative enough in privacy at Netherfield. You never seem at a loss for words, now, with me. You do not hate Society. You simply crave more intimate gatherings with your friends."

Darcy felt the corners of his lips turn up. He had never known anyone else to understand him so well. Even Bingley seemed unaware of Darcy's hatred of crowded events. He knew Bingley thought he was an amiable host by arranging activities for his guests, but Darcy would have preferred quiet evenings at the house. A thought struck him, causing his tentative smile to slip.

"What is it?" Elizabeth asked.

"I fear after growing up in such a busy household, you will find me and Pemberley quite boring."

"I would never find you boring." She smiled. "Do you know that I could not cease thinking about you and attempting to puzzle you out from our first meeting?"

"Did you really?" He knew she had not thought of him the way he thought of her, but knowing that she had thought of him at all pleased him.

"Yes," Elizabeth said as she turned her sparkling eyes to his. "I heard your words about me and wanted to hate you. I had to search deep and hard to find other reasons to dislike you. Not a day went by that your name was not on my tongue as I talked with a friend. Poor Jane and Charlotte must have tired of me. They must have seen through to the truth long before I ever did."

"The truth?"

"I was utterly obsessed with you."

"Why was that?"

"I do not know, but fortunately I have the rest of my life to find out."

"Do you know I was just as enchanted?" Darcy reached forward to stroke Elizabeth's smooth cheek.

"I thought you only looked at me to criticise."

"At first I had hoped to find faults. The more I looked, the more attracted I became."

"So it was my arts and allurements after all?" Elizabeth gave a coy smile.

"No, it was the spark in your eyes, the tone of your laughter, the smoothness of your skin, the lusciousness of your lips—"

Darcy could contain himself no longer. He sampled her lips, now parted in invitation. After several minutes, he pulled back. "I still find it difficult to believe that you are here with me, in my arms, and willing to marry me." He hung his head for a moment. "I know you do not love me, and I fear one day you will regret this union. I know you think that you bring nothing to this marriage, but you offer so much. Anything I can give you in return is not what you desire. My wealth and jewels mean nothing to you."

Elizabeth sighed and nuzzled into the hand which still touched her cheek. "You offer me what I desire above all else, Fitzwilliam."

"What is that?" Stability? A home?

"You," she whispered. "All I want is your love."

Darcy's heart swelled at her words and the look in her eyes. Perhaps she was too timid to say the words he longed to hear. Maybe she needed more time, but it made him hope as he never had before. He expressed himself the only way he could, and they were locked in mutually pleasurable pursuit until they arrived at a coaching inn.

No private dining room was available, so they sat in the large, common dining area of the tavern. Darcy observed Elizabeth to see if it brought back any bad memories of her recent employment. Instead, she encouraged them to mingle with other customers and play a singing game of who knew the most Scottish reels.

"I did not think you would know so many," Elizabeth whispered in his ear after they won the tenth round.

"I asked you to dance while Miss Bingley played a reel. Did you forget?"

"I had thought you meant to mock me." Elizabeth shook her head. "I should have guessed differently once I began to think differently of you."

"Dance with me now," he said and tugged on her hand.

"What? Here?" Elizabeth looked around the room. "Before all these strangers? Has the ale gone to your head?"

"Not at all," Darcy said as he stood. "Mr. William Smith wishes to dance with his lovely bride. Won't you, Lizzy?"

Elizabeth blushed, but Darcy could see that he pleased her. Others soon joined in, and they had a merry time until they were forced to sit out and catch their breath. Mindful that they needed to arise early to continue their journey, they soon said goodbyes to their new friends and ascended the stairs.

"Thank you for tonight," Elizabeth said once they were in bed and she was nestled in Darcy's arms.

"What did I do?"

"You were so carefree. You mingled with people far beneath you. Was it not for my sake?" She kissed him on the cheek.

"It was as much for my own as for yours," he answered with a grin.

"You see, you do not hate people as much as you would like to say."

"I think it is as you said this morning. I enjoy quality time with those I love. We may have been in a group of others, but I knew your focus was entirely on me." Darcy leaned forward to capture her lips.

"Oh, did you now?" Elizabeth ducked her head away.

"I can hardly believe it, but as I am helpless but to watch you no matter which room I am in, I know very well how often you, in turn, were watching me."

Elizabeth blushed, and Darcy kissed one rosy cheek. "I watched you even in Hertfordshire," she admitted.

"I know." Darcy nodded. "However, it is different now. I know the signs of your affection. I know the soft look your gaze takes when you are pleased with me. How I could take your expression from those months ago to mean admiration is proof enough of my arrogance and conceit."

"Hush," Elizabeth said. "Do not think of those times. Let us think only of now. We are here together." She gripped him tightly. "I will always be with you."

Darcy welcomed Elizabeth's kisses and responded in kind. She melted at his touch and moulded herself to his body. At that moment, Darcy knew that she would allow him to touch every curve, every inch of her smooth skin. However, he had promised both of them that he would not claim her until she was in love with him. Until she could say the words and speak of her heart, he would have to resist. Slowing their kisses and his hands' explorations, he laid her head on his shoulder and held her while their breathing returned to normal and they both fell asleep.

When they reached the inn on their third night of travel, a letter had arrived for Elizabeth.

"It is from Jane." She reverently stroked the

script. "I would know her writing anywhere, but it did not come from Longbourn. How interesting."

"Let us hurry to our room, and you may read it there."

"You do not wish to eat first?"

"We will have refreshments brought to us."

Elizabeth's smile was thanks enough. Once she was settled, she began reading aloud.

Dearest Lizzy,

Undoubtedly, you are curious about the address from which this letter was posted. This might shock you, but given your own good news about a match with Mr. Darcy, I am sure you will not resent it. I have married.

Elizabeth paused to gasp and bring her hand to her mouth. "Oh, Janie."

"Does she say to whom she is wed?"

Elizabeth returned her eyes to the paper and began reading once more.

After you left, I met a gentleman with an estate about ten miles from Meryton. We had not met before because he had spent the last five years in Bath for his wife's illness. She died last year, and he returned to his estate to complete his mourning. He had an acquaintance with Sir William Lucas, and we met during an evening at Lucas Lodge. Mr. Nash is exceptionally amiable, and while he had not spent much time in Hertfordshire in the last ten years, he quickly resumed his friendships in the Meryton area. We met many times for some weeks, and eventually he made me an offer.

Mama is beside herself as his income is nearly equal to Mr. Bingley's and certainly more than Mr. Collins's. I suppose you would say there is some advantage to having Mama further away than the few miles between Longbourn and Netherfield. However, I must tell you that I do believe you misunderstood my feelings. I was not nearly as overwrought as you seem to think. I resorted to the laudanum only to sleep, and due to my long fatigue, I must have taken more than I should have.

Elizabeth ceased reading and gasped. "That is not true at all!"

Darcy captured Elizabeth's hand in his.

"She had not been sleeping, that is correct. However, she did quite intentionally take too much laudanum. She confessed it to me. She wanted it all to end."

Elizabeth turned watery eyes on Darcy, and his heart broke for her. Jane's desire to erase Elizabeth's memory of an embarrassing moment for her was understandable. He did not think Jane intentionally wounded Elizabeth in her need for self-preservation, but she was injured all the same. He pulled Elizabeth into his arms. "Dearest, I believe you."

"According to this testimony, I left Longbourn for no reason. Jane was not ill. It was not wrong of our parents to refuse her help. She makes my sacrifices into ridiculous selfishness.

I am no better than Kitty and Lydia."

"Is that what you truly think?"

Elizabeth cried quietly for several minutes on Darcy's shoulder as he stroked her back. Finally, she lifted her head and met his gaze. "I know the facts. I can see that Jane is putting forth this version to hide her own hurt, and she feels ashamed of her actions. She should not, of course. I can also see that Kitty and Lydia left not because they were wicked but as an attempt to salvage their lives somehow. I only wish we knew where Lydia was."

"We will find her, love. As soon as we marry, we will begin our search."

"It would require communication with my father. I did not think you would prefer that."

Darcy frowned. "It is true that I cannot respect the man and certainly cannot understand his actions. However, I wish to find and assist your sister almost as desperately as you do."

"You truly are the best of men," Elizabeth said with a sad smile.

"You know I am not. I have flaws, and I will not let you forget them. I could not even if I tried. Whatever good you see in my helping Lydia is from knowing you." Would he ever find the right words to convince her that she made him a better man? "What else does Jane say? Do you feel ready to continue?"

Elizabeth nodded and resumed reading aloud.

We married about a month ago, and Mary resides with us. So you see, there is no cause to worry for Mary or me or hasten to Longbourn. We, however, fear for you.

Elizabeth blushed and ceased reading.

"What is it?" Darcy asked.

"She cites my former dislike of you. I thought I was profuse enough in my praise in the letter I sent, but perhaps I was not. I will amend that in the reply."

Her eyes returned to the paper she held and continued to scan. "Mama and Papa were very angry at my departure. You were correct." She met Darcy's eyes. "They claimed I was suddenly sent to London. When the Gardiners did not find me at the inn, they returned home rather than arrive in Meryton. They were the ones who came up with the suggestion that I was with them."

Elizabeth blinked back tears. "They had searched for Lydia and Kitty for so long. I suppose they tired of the Bennets' follies. Or perhaps they were out of money."

Darcy wrapped Elizabeth in an embrace. "What are you thinking, love?"

"I am worth less to them somehow. They love me less. If my own flesh and blood can do so..."

"I will silence those thoughts." He pressed a kiss to her temple, her cheek, and, finally, her eyelids. "I cannot say why they gave up the search for you. I would leave no stone unturned to find you. You are more precious to me than my own heart."

168

Darcy captured Elizabeth's lips for good measure. Drawing back, he nestled her head against his shoulder and stroked her arm. "What do you wish to do?"

Unexpectedly, she turned her head and pressed a kiss to his jaw. "Can you show me what love is again, Fitzwilliam?"

Darcy pulled her to her feet and scooped her up in his arms.

"Your arm!" she cried as she wrapped her own around his neck.

"It is much recovered, like your ankle." He laid her on the bed and brought her hand to rest over his heart. "Our injuries mended together as our hearts have. As long as I live, I will love you."

Elizabeth kissed Darcy with a desperation which inflamed his passions. It was still three days until they reached Scotland, and his honour had never been in greater danger. Judging by the pleased smile Elizabeth wore and her restful slumber, she had no complaints at all about the way he showed his love.

Chapter Fourteen

Over the next few days, Elizabeth thought much about Jane's letter. She had replied the following day. Uncertain how to approach Jane's presentation of her illness, Elizabeth avoided addressing the past at Longbourn. Instead, she congratulated Jane on her marriage and reiterated her blossoming feelings for Darcy.

Soon, she would need to explain to Jane the change in her understanding—not about Darcy but about herself and her family. That would be best to do in person, however, so Elizabeth decided to bide her time. She had no doubts regarding Darcy's character and intended to tell her sister so. More importantly, Elizabeth knew she would have a healthy future, for she chose to heal. Jane's insistence in pushing away her mental strain and redefining her feelings and actions worried Elizabeth. She knew it was impossible for Jane to merely wake up entirely new and healed the next morning and skip down the sunny lanes of Meryton and into the arms of a Prince Charming. Happily ever after was possible, of course, but the dragons must be defeated first. Judging from her letter, Jane acted as though there was nothing to vanquish.

The days and nights with Darcy furthered their intimacy. Elizabeth still wished for moments of greater privacy and a greater variety of activities. She was ever so tired of carriages and inns. Darcy had kept his promise, however, and arranged for her to have time to walk in the middle of the day. They would have a light repast and then walk about whatever village or town they were in before returning to the carriage.

Her time with Darcy brought to mind her own deficiencies. It was allowable that she not have any other pursuit while travelling, but Elizabeth noticed she had no activity to occupy her when they stopped in the evenings. She had always thought she used her time wisely and that her parents were sensible in not pushing their daughters to learn things which did not appeal to them. However, now she saw how ill-prepared she was for anything beyond being the daughter of a gentleman of middle means. She believed she could speak with the housekeeper and handle her tasks for the estate fine enough. If the rest of her life was merely attempting witty conversation at dinner parties, she could perform those duties well. What she sorely lacked, though, was knowledge in how to exist in quiet moments with a reserved man.

She did not mind the silence, of course. She was curious enough to read about current affairs and intelligent enough to converse with her betrothed about them. It was the other times that she did not know what to do. At Longbourn, there had always been a sister with whom to talk or argue. There was always some conflict to ignore, watch, or attempt to stop. The lack of distress and crisis made Elizabeth decidedly restless and nervous. Perhaps if she embroidered or painted fireplace screens, she would have some activity to take her mind off such things.

Darcy did not seem to mind. In fact, he appeared inordinately pleased merely to be in the same room as her, even if they were silent for much of the time and occupied in separate pursuits. Elizabeth supposed much of her life at Pemberley would be this way. Suddenly, a thought occurred to her. At Longbourn, she acted as she did out of a need for survival. She did not enjoy those mindless accomplishments thrust upon most ladies, but even if she did, she would not have been able to study them to mastery. There was too much conflict in her home. Indeed, much of her character relied on who she had to be for her family. She must direct her sisters. She must share in her father's jokes. She must not cringe at her mother's vulgarity. She must not partake of her sisters' frivolity too much, nor be as severe as Mary. She should not be as kind as Jane, who was easily taken advantage of.

Who was Elizabeth Bennet without her family? The thought which used to anger or terrify her suddenly felt like great freedom. She could be absolutely anyone she wanted. And what was more, she knew that Darcy would love her unconditionally.

He looked up from his book just as the realisation struck her. She was saved from having to explain the queer expression in her eyes by the carriage jostling over a rock.

"We should make it to Holyhead before nightfall," he said.

Excitement brimmed in Elizabeth. At Holyhead, they would board a ship to ferry them to Scotland. They would marry at Portpatrick and then journey to Ireland before they returned to Pemberley.

Despite Elizabeth's desire to arrive in time to tour the coastal town, they reached the inn as darkness blanketed the sky. The last several miles of road were rough and required a slower pace. Even then, the carriage was stuck in a rut twice and required the men to push it out. Elizabeth let out a sigh that her first view of the seaside was not during daylight or even the romance of the sunset. Clouds covered much of the sky, meaning there were very few visible stars to reflect on the water and it was unsafe to walk on the promenade. Darcy had promised, however, that they could rise early the next day. Elizabeth supposed seeing the sunrise was fair enough compensation.

When they entered the coaching inn, he needed to speak with the inn's proprietor about a few matters. Elizabeth was shown to their room by a maid. Unexpectedly, she returned a few moments later with a letter in hand. Elizabeth thought she made out Jane's new address, but the writing was not as neat as usual. Tearing it open, Elizabeth stumbled into a chair as she read the words.

Dearest Lizzy,

I have directed this letter to Holyhead in hopes that it will reach you before you board your ship for Scotland. I have just come from Longbourn and have been urged to send for you.

About a week ago, Papa was injured riding over the fields. He had fallen from his horse, and it was many hours before anyone found him. He sustained a head injury and a severe break to the leg. His pain was acute but more troubling was the amount of blood he had lost. It was evident, too, to the men who found him that his leg could not be saved. We sent for the apothecary and surgeon. They agreed an amputation was necessary.

They had hoped for a quick recovery, but Papa was too weak from the blood loss. After several days of fever, a physician was sent for. He arrived earlier today and has observed Papa all day. He has given us no reason to hope.

I know your differences with our parents. I can even understand you blaming them for Kitty and Lydia's elopements. However, no matter their faults, they are our parents. If you hasten, you might have some time with Papa before he passes. Either way, your presence will be a balm to our mother. They have lost two daughters already. Will you make them lose another?

--Jane

Elizabeth's mind raced. She could be ready in an instant. They could be on the road again in less than an hour. Surely Darcy could arrange for them to travel overnight, and they might arrive at Longbourn in less time than it took for them on the first journey. He would support her.

As soon as the thought crept in, she dismissed it. Darcy had every reason to think ill of the Bennets. He would never condone Elizabeth cancelling their plans to see to her wayward parents. Indeed, he never would conscience to see them again. He had admitted only to a willingness to write to Mr. Bennet about how to help find Lydia. He had made no promises to visit Longbourn or to personally search for her. Mr. Bennet would soon die, and she doubted Darcy would be willing to communicate with Mrs. Bennet. Even more, he would not get a sensible reply. Darcy surely esteemed Mr. Gardiner even less than the Bennets, between his lower rank and the greater pain the couple had caused Elizabeth.

There also was the continued issue of propriety. It was one matter to elope. It was another to spend weeks together unchaperoned and at inns without marriage. She would be no better than Lydia at that point. Gossip could hardly be avoided if she arrived at Longbourn unmarried. If he accompanied her, it would taint him and possibly even his sister, who had been through enough.

Besides all this, he would feel any request to alter their plans to be an abandonment of him. He would feel jilted. He had sacrificed so much for her, and she would be just as well as leaving him behind. Oh, he would be too honourable and selfless to say anything. He might even accompany her all the way to Longbourn. However, it would burn in their relationship. Once at Longbourn, she would be at the mercy of her mother's grief. All the expectations would weigh on her.

Jane and Mary had become ill once before and might again under stress. What would happen if they succumbed again and Elizabeth was not there to assist them? She could hardly hope they— or even herself—would be able to behave perfectly. Something would invariably happen that would separate her from Darcy. He would see why she was so unsuitable and come to his senses at last.

Elizabeth understood that if she desired to return to Longbourn, she would be as good as ending her relationship with Darcy. As such, she should finish it now rather than prolong the pain. She would need to rescind her agreement to marry him and flee. The heartbreak was impossible to avoid, and it was better to face it on her own terms.

Two choices were before her: Return to her family or marry Darcy.

"Here we are, my love," Darcy said as he opened the door.

Elizabeth hastily shoved the letter under the folds of her gown. Two servants walked in behind him carrying trays of refreshments and tea. He motioned for them to set them down on the table near Elizabeth. He sat in the chair opposite her.

After the servants left, he inquired about which items she would prefer and served her.

Elizabeth found she had little appetite. Her mind considered how she might do what needed to be done. Could she bear to see the heartbreak in his eyes as she chose her family over him? Could she bear knowing that she was forever separating herself from perhaps the only person in the world who could love and respect her so unconditionally?

"You are quiet this evening," Darcy observed after Elizabeth had either not heard or delayed in answering three or four of his questions.

A knock sounded at the door, and Darcy bade them enter. A maid appeared with wine, and Elizabeth's eyes lit up. Yes, if Darcy would imbibe enough, she could leave while he slept. She would leave a note for him to find in the morning.

Elizabeth jumped when he placed a hand on her shoulder. She looked at him in surprise. When had he left his chair?

"Are you well, Elizabeth?"

"I suppose it was the journey today. I am more tired than usual."

"I am not surprised," he said. "I ordered the wine in case you required it."

He handed her a glass, and she took it with a tense smile.

"You have barely touched your food." He frowned at her plate. "Perhaps you need rest more than anything else."

Elizabeth leaned forward to take a biscuit so he might fret over her less. She had never deserved his goodness. The movement caused the letter to crinkle underneath her gown.

Darcy eyed her curiously, and then his eyes fell on a scrap that she had torn in her hasty opening. It had dropped on the floor. "Did you get a letter?"

Elizabeth nodded and held her breath, searching to find something to say.

"From Jane again? What did she have to say so soon? I would be surprised if she even got your reply before this was sent."

"I would prefer not to speak about it at present," Elizabeth said with an exhale.

Darcy's hand left her shoulder. He caressed up her neck before lifting her chin with his thumb and forefinger. "No wonder you seem downcast this evening." He placed a kiss on her forehead.

Elizabeth nearly whimpered at the gesture. "My stomach is unsettled. I do not think I should have the wine," she said and glanced at the carafe. "You must be exhausted from helping with the carriage. Please, drink as you please."

"I would not wish for you to think I am a drunkard."

"I will worry about you otherwise," she said, and it was not the lie she had intended.

Darcy's affectionate and grateful look pulled on her heart more than anything else. He looked so pleased to see a sign of her regard. What was she doing? Why was she willing to leave the man she loved?

The realisation made her still as Darcy refilled his glass. She loved him as she had never loved another. She loved him without reserve and without fear. She was not entirely sure what he would say or do regarding her sister's request, but Elizabeth realised her thoughts had been flawed. He would not condemn her for wishing to be with her family. He would not reject her or even make her choose between them. She thought that even if the worst was said about their elopement and it tainted his good name, he would still stand by her. The man practically lived to make her happy and had sacrificed so much for her.

No, it was not Darcy who would make her choose between him and her family. How had it not occurred to Jane that requesting Elizabeth to return unmarried would likely forever ruin the possibilities of it? Perhaps Jane supposed that mattered little to Elizabeth after the months she spent away from Longbourn, but a woman with a botched elopement could not be Mrs. Darcy. Elizabeth thought too highly of the Darcy name and loved him too much to make him live with a tarnished legacy. Once rumours started, who knew what they would contain? Before too long they would hit upon something so close to the truth that it would remind someone of a memory. Some passing traveller would have seen her at the inn. From there it would be easy to assume she had prostituted herself, and then all their efforts to conceal her identity would be ruined. Marrying Darcy only worked if she could do so honourably and without destroying his name.

"Come," Darcy said as he put his glass down. He walked to Elizabeth and took her hands in his, raising them up to assist her in standing. "I will leave so you may get ready for bed. We want an early start tomorrow."

"Of course," Elizabeth said with a tremulous smile. "For the ship."

"Yes, I would not want to miss that. It is not every day I plan to sail to Scotland to marry my love. However, I meant so you may view the sunrise over the sea." He kissed her forehead again before departing.

The kiss sealed it. She could not forsake him. She loved him too much. Lord forgive her, but she could not choose her family over Darcy, over them, or over her. She had genuine love and happiness before her, and she would take hold of it with both hands.

Chapter Fifteen

Elizabeth waited behind the folding screen in the room of the Jester's Inn. She focused on taking deep breaths despite the hammering in her chest. A faint breeze drifted from the barely open window. Salt air filled her nostrils, calming and tantalizing in equal measures. Soon she would begin on a journey crossing the sea, and she knew her heart had just started its journey in loving Darcy.

How had she not seen it all earlier? This week must have been torturous for Darcy as she kept him at arm's length. It was only testament to how hurt she had been when they met again that she feared she could love no one—not even him. Now that she realised it, she could barely wait to tell him and launch herself into his arms. Nervously, she shifted her weight from foot to foot waiting for him to appear.

In due time, Darcy knocked on the door, and Elizabeth called for him to enter. She could hear him come into the chamber, then shut and lock the entrance. Unable to see, her ears were more alert than ever to the now familiar sounds of her beloved readying for the evening. There was a gentle scraping sound as he placed his cufflinks on a table. Next, he sat and tugged off his boots before removing his coat and waistcoat.

The noises of Darcy removing his clothing sent goose pimples over Elizabeth's skin and made her breath catch. In the silence, she could even hear the fabric of his cravat thread through his fingers. He had been without his valet since they left London. Aside from dressing himself, his whiskers were growing out and Elizabeth secretly loved look.

On their first night after reaching Town, Elizabeth was too timid to watch Darcy disrobe. He came to bed in his shirtsleeves and breeches, which seemed unbearably intimate. Elizabeth had hidden her face while he discarded his garments. In recent days, she had grown bolder, sneaking peeks at him now and then. She could imagine him now, although she could not see him.

Finally, he stood, and the moment of truth had arrived.

"Elizabeth?"

She could hear the confusion in his voice.

"Where are you?"

"I—I am here," she said from behind the screen. Her voice shook.

"Is anything wrong? Do you need assistance?" He stepped towards her.

"I am perfectly well. Stay where you are."

Hearing his obedience, Elizabeth exhaled and emerged from behind the screen. She stared at her feet until Darcy's quick exhale brought her eyes to his. Quickly, he averted them.

"Forgive me—I—I—I thought you were ready for me to enter."

"Fitzwilliam, look at me."

"Pardon, you are—you are—"

What she could see of one cheek was bright red. His embarrassment and shyness at her nudity were so endearing. She took a bold step forward. The sound of her movement made him begin to turn his head before he snapped it away again. At the closer proximity, she could see how rapidly his chest rose and fell. His hands tensed at his side as though he were forcing them to remain there. His posture was taut, reminding her of a string pulled to its maximum and about to snap.

"I want you to look at me."

Again, his head began to move, but he would not turn it all the way. A muscle in his neck twitched. "You do?"

"Very much," Elizabeth said as she took another step. She was close enough to touch him now.

Slowly, he turned his head. His eyes widened, and a look of utter fascination and delight filled them. She stood as he perused her body, his eyes dropping over specific contours and curves before returning to her gaze. The tension in his body remained.

She ought to feel timid or ashamed. However, she could see his appreciation. She had never felt more beautiful. The feeling did not emerge because this honourable man loved her or looked at her with undeniable desire in his eyes. She felt beautiful because she finally loved herself. She accepted her flaws and could see her strengths. What more could she ask to be in life than a woman who fiercely loved? After a long moment of unspoken communication, she broke their silence.

"I want you to see me now, bare before you, as you have always seen my heart." She reached for one of his hands and pressed it to her heart, and Darcy let out a shuddery breath. "I love you, Fitzwilliam. I love you with my whole heart, and you have shown me that it is not absent or numb or shattered. It finally knows what it is to love and be loved because of you."

She raised his hand to her lips and tried to pour all her love into her gaze as their eyes remained connected. "I have nothing to my name. According to Society, my future would be desolate and as exposed as my body now is. However, if you will have me, I offer my heart for as long as you or I shall live."

"You love me?"

Elizabeth nodded as Darcy's hopeful look turned to disbelief before being replaced entirely by joy. "I love you."

Darcy's restraint was gone. He pulled her into his arms for a sizzling kiss and held her so close that she could feel his heart beat against her skin. His hands roamed over her body. "We will wed tomorrow." Darcy panted between breaths when he broke their kiss. "There is no rush to—"

"I trust you." She wrapped her arms around his neck and pressed herself further against him.

Darcy let out a strangled moan as his lips fell to her neck. Her legs buckled as glorious sensation swept over her body. Darcy caught her in his arms and carried her to their bed.

Darcy murmured words of love into Elizabeth's ear, causing her mind to empty of everything but this moment. When he kissed down her neck and his fingers began gentle caresses over her body, she grew dizzy. Settled against the pillows, she opened her arms, welcomed Darcy into her heart, and placed her body into his loving care.

Darcy awoke to the feeling of Elizabeth's exploratory and inviting touch as she caressed the thick patch of hair at the top of his chest. She seemed entirely fascinated with what he had always considered a rather unremarkable part of his anatomy. He feigned sleep to see how far her curiosity would take her.

The evening before, his wildest fantasies came true. Elizabeth loved him and displayed her trust in him with more courage than he thought likely to be found in most men. A night of spine-tingling pleasure ensued. Yet this evening promised even more, as he had shocked even himself by withholding full consummation of their love until their marriage could be legally condoned.

However, Elizabeth began pressing kisses to his chest, her head trailing lower and his resolve quickly vanishing.

"If you continue that, we will not only miss the sunrise but our ship as well. I might never let you out of this bed again," he said to her in a husky voice as he opened one eye.

She moved her head to look at him, her curls trailing over his skin, making him tense at the pleasure. Elizabeth blushed, but her eyes danced with merriment.

"We already missed the sunrise."

"Did we?" Darcy leaned up on his elbows to see the window on the other side of the room. "I am sorry. I had wanted your first glimpse of the sea to be spectacular."

Elizabeth's lips turned up in a pleased smile before she kissed his stomach, allowing her tongue to briefly lave over the skin. Darcy slumped back in the bed. "Lizzy." He did not know if he was warning her or begging her.

Her head popped back up. "As it happens, I cannot complain about my morning. I can view the sea at sunrise some other time. I would not trade this moment with you for the world's most splendid vista."

Darcy tugged on Elizabeth's arm, bringing her lips to his. She cut the kiss far shorter than he would have preferred.

"Let us ready for the day, Fitzwilliam," she said. "I am most eager to become Mrs. Darcy."

Darcy could think of a hundred pleasurable things that would keep them in bed for a week, but he could think of nothing better than making her his wife this very day. "And so the ordering about begins already?"

"Of course." Elizabeth smirked as she climbed out of bed. "I plan to be a most proper wife."

Darcy frowned, and Elizabeth laughed at his expression. "Have your laugh now, but you will see that I rule my household firmly. I will not be nagged by my wife into doing all her bidding." He got out of bed and immediately reached for her.

Elizabeth laughingly danced away from his reach. "Dearest Fitzwilliam. I have a much better plan than to nag you to death."

"Do you?" he asked as he followed after her. She was all playful movements, and he moved more like a cat on the prowl. "What will you do?" he asked as Elizabeth reached a wall and Darcy leaned both arms on either side of her head.

"Oh, I will convince you with sweetness instead."

"I am not so easily swayed," he murmured against her ear, smiling at her shiver in response. "Now, perhaps a kiss..."

"A kiss?" Elizabeth's tone belied astonishment. She pulled his head down to her level and whispered in his ear. "I had planned on seduction."

Before Darcy could reward her bold impertinence, she ducked out from under his arms and chuckled as she danced away again.

"Why are you over there if that is your intention?" Darcy asked, the pout on his lips very real.

"I have to be your wife first, silly." Elizabeth grinned. "Come, we must make haste. I am afraid our lovemaking last night tired us out."

As she slipped behind the screen to dress, Darcy marvelled not only at her lingering modesty but that he had never heard so many statements which could lighten his heart in such a short time. Elizabeth loved him, she could not wait to marry him, and she delighted in making love. By the time they had left their room, he could not stop grinning. He reckoned no man who saw Elizabeth would need to wonder at the cause of his joy.

They packed the few items they needed for the evening and were on their way. Despite Elizabeth's anxiety, they arrived with enough time to allow them a brief excursion along the promenade. Darcy smiled hearing Elizabeth's oohs and ahhs at the sights. The morning sun dazzled on the sea; the clouds of the night before had vanished. She relished the breeze on her face and the smell of the salt air. He could hardly contain his mirth at her expression when they approached the harbour.

"They are much larger than I had expected."

"This is good." Darcy chuckled. He would hardly like to cross the sea with his bride on nothing sturdier than a fishing vessel. "Had you never seen the docks in London?"

Elizabeth replied that she had not, and he considered again how sheltered her life had been. He relished the opportunity to give her new experiences.

"Are you scared at all?" he whispered as they boarded the ship. He thought he detected a tremor in her hand as it rested on his arm.

"Not with you here," she said, squeezing his arm.

Despite her brave words, Darcy believed she carried some anxiety and knew it was perfectly ordinary. The journey to Portpatrick was only a few hours, and the ship had no cabins for the passengers. The few vessels which attempted longer sea travel—always a dangerous venture made worse by Napoleon—offered places to sleep. Their ship offered only a large common room, leaving the cabins for the crew and much of the area for cargo.

As the ship set sail, Darcy and Elizabeth stood on the deck and watched as Holyhead's harbour grew smaller and smaller. Having been on a ship a few times to travel to Scotland and Ireland, Darcy adjusted to the rolling sensation. A glance at Elizabeth assured him that she did not fare as well. Escorting her to the common area, he found a seat for her and offered some refreshment, which she refused.

"Is it her first time on a ship?" a friendly voice said to Darcy's right.

Elizabeth nodded, a bit shyly, Darcy thought, at the lady.

"Ah, I remember my first time. The sickness always hits me but not nearly so bad as the first time. All I can promise you is that you don't die from it, and we are in safe hands with Captain Harvey. It will all be worth it in the end," she said as only the old and wise can. "Scotland is a beauty. It's proof that God can paint as well as any Master."

"No one said she had never been to Scotland before," the gentleman next to her harrumphed.

"Oh! I suppose you are correct, my dear," the lady bubbled. "Well, have you been to Scotland before, missus? What brings you to journey there?"

Darcy and Elizabeth glanced at each other and blushed. They had not rehearsed what to say if asked such a thing. Darcy had not thought it likely to be approached in such a fashion.

"Harriet, mind your tongue," the man said. "You have embarrassed them. Why do you think two young people are going to Scotland?"

"Goodness!" She glanced at them, eyeing the way Elizabeth's hand rested in Darcy's, nearly leaning on him for support as the long bench provided none for her back. "Pray, forgive me. I am not usually so chattery. My nerves get the best of me on a ship, you see. However, I had thought you must be a married couple of some years. She seems to rely on you so and trust you implicitly."

With such an observation, Darcy and Elizabeth blushed again, but he could not be displeased.

The woman's husband leaned forward and spoke in softer tones. "Do not mind us. We do not judge you in the least. We ran away together thirty years ago, and it has been the best decision I ever made."

"I should say so, Mr. Scott!" The woman chuckled. "We go back now to visit our daughter. She has married a clergyman who resides in Glasgow. We could sail all the way there, but I prefer to spend the least amount of time on a ship as possible. Of course, it will all be worth it to see the baby."

"My congratulations," Elizabeth offered with a smile.

The two couples chatted amiably for the course of the journey, Darcy noting that Elizabeth seemed to perk up from the conversation.

"Oh, I wish my Agnes could meet you," Mrs. Scott said to Elizabeth as the ship docked. "If ever you two are in Glasgow, you must visit Mr. and Mrs. David Russell in Parkhead. I am sure you both would just adore little Johnny. What a bright one he is already!"

Darcy smiled as the lady affectionately babbled on about her grandson. Her husband added his own pieces until they had to depart from the ship. The couple seemed lower in status than him and were far more outgoing than he typically preferred, but they were amiable and kind. Additionally, he could see the enduring love between the two, and it was impossible for him not to wish that thirty years hence he and Elizabeth might be just as in love and enamoured of a grandchild. When Mrs. Scott asked to correspond with Elizabeth, Darcy wholeheartedly supported Elizabeth's resounding yes.

Directing a young man to send their trunks to the appropriate inn, Darcy and Elizabeth walked to the nearest church, although not required by law, and pledged their troth. Assured of a legal and consecrated marriage, they ended the day in each other's arms, finally one in body and soul.

Chapter Sixteen

It was three days before Darcy or Elizabeth turned their thoughts to leaving the Portpatrick Inn.

"Do you still wish to see Ireland? It would require more ships, but I think you tolerated it well, all in all," Darcy said over their private breakfast on the fourth day after they had married.

Elizabeth hung her head and chewed her bottom lip. It had been such a relief over the last few days to ignore all the problems with her family and just live for herself.

"Or we could go straight to Pemberley."

Elizabeth did not reply and did not need to seek Darcy's eyes to know he was looking at her and attempting to read her expression.

After several minutes of silence, Darcy asked in a voice just above a whisper, "Are you regretting our marriage?"

"What?" Elizabeth's head bobbed up, and she threw her arms around him as they sat next to one another on a settee. "No, never that!" She pressed kisses to his face as tears filled her eyes.

"Then what are you afraid to tell me?"

Elizabeth sighed. She should have known he would pick up on her reticence. She should have guessed that he would feel hurt. "Before we left Holyhead, I had a letter from Jane."

"Yes, I recall. You did not wish to discuss it."

"She told me that our father was on his deathbed. He most assuredly is dead by now. She asked me to return to Longbourn."

"She asked for your return or attempted to manipulate it?"

"I am not quite sure," Elizabeth confessed. "You can read it for yourself." She retrieved the letter from a valise. "I do not think Jane would intentionally manipulate me; however, it hurts not to be sure. You can see, though, that I made my choice."

Darcy scanned over Elizabeth's letter and thought for a few moments before replying. "What do you wish to do now? We could go to Longbourn, and you could pay your respects to your father. I assume your mother is provided for?"

Elizabeth nodded. "Despite all of Mama's fears, I know she had a competent jointure. Mary is welcome to live with Jane. Her income will be more than enough just for herself." She blew out a long breath. "I suppose I do not know what I want to do. I feel as though I am supposed to return, as though it is a duty or expectation."

"Do you fear what others will think or say if you do not go?"

Elizabeth shrugged. "Is that so wrong of me?"

"Right and wrong are not at stake. If you feel in your heart it is the right thing to do, then do not dismiss it. But if you only feel pulled to go because it might displease others of no consequence to yourself, then I would say it is harmful." He reached for Elizabeth's hand. "However, I will support you either way. I would not have you go alone."

"Thank you," Elizabeth said and squeezed his hand. "I worry about my sisters and how they might bear the weight. However, it is not my role to save them. Jane is married now and perfectly in her rights to employ her time with her husband. Mama's situation of losing her husband is pitiable, but I cannot heal her heart—if indeed her heart is touched at all. I will continue to communicate with Jane and begin writing to Mary. I can always visit later. It is better to begin how I mean to continue."

"Very well, love." He pulled Elizabeth to him and kissed her forehead. "So, do you wish to journey to Ireland or Pemberley?"

"I know we are far closer to Ireland than we will likely be at any other time and I do wish to see it someday, but I think I would very much like to go to Pemberley. I just want to go home with you."

Elizabeth cuddled close to Darcy for the remainder of the morning. In the afternoon, they explored the port. Then Darcy arranged for them to rent a carriage for their trip to Pemberley. They left the following morning and arrived in Dumfries before dinner on their second day of travel. While dining in the coaching inn, a man stared strangely at Elizabeth.

Before he left, he paused at their table. "A fine performance you gave a few nights ago, Miss Lucks."

"I beg your pardon." Darcy stood so suddenly that his knee hit the table, jostling the silverware. "My wife is not an actress."

"I mean no offence, sir," the man said with raised palms. "She looks very much like Miss Angelina Maria Lucks, who I saw only a few nights ago." He turned a truly remorseful face to Elizabeth. "I ask for your forgiveness, missus. You do look remarkably like her."

Elizabeth blushed but said, "All is forgiven, sir. I bid you good evening."

The man nodded and walked on. Darcy took his seat, and the meal resumed as best it could. However, Elizabeth turned over what the man had said. When they returned to their room, she spoke her thoughts to her husband.

"I think, dearest, that man might have spoken of Lydia."

"Do you think she would be an actress?" Darcy sounded shocked.

"It surprises me no less than her elopement did. She followed reports of many actresses in the gossip columns. She loved putting on plays when we were children. She and Maria Lucas sometimes made their dolls into actresses. Maria always chose the name Maria Lucks. I could see Lydia poking fun by borrowing her friend's never-to-be-realised stage name. Additionally, she would have had very few options available to her after Wickham's abandonment. People have often said we looked very similar. Although," Elizabeth added with a sad smile, "she always enjoyed letting everyone know she was taller."

"Do you wish to see her?"

Elizabeth had a ready answer. "First, it is worth knowing a bit more about this woman. I do not know how she would have made her way to Dumfries. It could also be that she is part of a travelling troupe and has already left. At any rate, I think I should not publicly approach her. I am sorry for your sake if she is on the stage."

"Why is that?"

"The wife of Mr. Darcy related to an actress?" Elizabeth shook her head. "The scandal!"

"I do not care about that at all," Darcy said. "I have told you I do not care about Society's opinions anymore. At any rate, some actresses become quite famous and nearly respectable. It would be far better for her to have a visible profession than the more likely alternative."

Elizabeth could only nod. "Then I suggest you ask about Angelina Maria Lucks. When we are home at Pemberley, you could arrange for a representative to speak with her. I do not suppose she would give up her career or think we should offer her an alternative. She could not return to Longbourn. However, it would mean the world to me to know that she was alive, healthy, and reasonably safe."

"An excellent plan, my love. Now I would much rather discuss Elizabeth Darcy than sisters or actresses."

"Me?"

"Yes." Darcy smiled seductively and leaned close to her ear. "There is no other woman worth discussing. Your beauty is unparalleled."

Elizabeth felt her face warm, and goose pimples covered her flesh. "You did not always think so."

"Do not quote the ignorant and foolish, my love."

He kissed just below her ear, causing a shiver to race through her body.

"That was when I only first knew you, and I know you far, far better now."

He kissed down the side of her neck, and Elizabeth angled her head to give him better access. He reached her collarbone and sucked. Elizabeth's toes curled, and a longing moan escaped her parted lips. "Fitzwilliam?"

"Yes, Elizabeth?" Darcy murmured against her flesh before continuing his exploration.

"Let us go to bed."

Darcy scooped Elizabeth into his arms and carried her across the room.

"We will arrive at the house in about five minutes," Darcy said as they turned up the drive to Pemberley two days later.

Elizabeth knew he could sense her anxiety. At first she had expressed nothing but a desire to see her new home and meet her new sister, but as they drew closer to their destination, she had confessed to being nervous. It was incredibly difficult for her to articulate her fears and misgivings.

Thankfully, Darcy responded with patience rather than presuming every self-doubt meant she regretted their marriage. He had praised her emotional strength and resiliency. Additionally, he acknowledged her hard work to overcome the crippling self-doubt and distrust which assailed her when they first met again. Darcy said she was one of the bravest people the world had ever known, and generals could only wish to have her courage.

"Are you still nervous about meeting the staff?" he asked as he took her hand in his. "Remember what I said. There is no pressure to take on any duty for which you do not care. I did not marry you so I could have someone run my estate. I love you just as you are."

Elizabeth gave him an encouraging smile. He knew just how to ease her fears. How had she ever worried he would regret marrying her? Even better than feeling comfortable in accepting his love, she realised that what she really sought was her own self-approval. She knew he would continue to support her in those healthy feelings. As such, all would be well no matter what the future held. It was fantastic to feel more carefree than she had in months.

She let out a happy sigh before meeting his eyes. "It is only fear of the unknown. I know there will be an adjustment period. I am determined, however, to keep myself happy first."

"I would not want it any other way," he said.

He did not ask and she did not feel the pressure to add that she would see to his happiness. She had worried, a little, that considering her own feelings first was selfish. However, she need not be a slave to her own emotions. There was no reason why she could not consider her happiness while taking care of her husband's feelings. She would not be like Mrs. Bennet, who never thought of anyone but herself.

"Here we are." Darcy tugged on her hand and pointed out the window as the wooded lane cleared, and they saw the mansion house situated behind the river they now approached.

"Oh!" Elizabeth breathed. "It is delightful!"

Darcy had turned his head to watch her reaction and smiled in response. He had told her she would like the grounds even more than the house, and until this moment she was not entirely sure he was correct. She grinned at the idea of soon knowing every path.

The carriage pulled up to the house, stopping in front of the great stone steps. Outside, the staff awaited their arrival as Georgiana and Mrs. Annesley stood at the top. Darcy shared a smile with Elizabeth before handing her out of the carriage. She was most pleased to note there was no tremble to her hand.

They stopped in front of the housekeeper first. The look in Darcy's eye as he gave the introductions and formally presented Elizabeth as Mrs. Darcy told her it was one of the highest honours of his life. Next, there was the reunion with Georgiana. After introducing Mrs. Annesley, Darcy addressed his sister.

She met him with nervous eyes, but he smiled adoringly at her. "Georgiana, may I present your new sister and my wife, Elizabeth Darcy?"

"I am very pleased to meet you, Mrs. Darcy." Georgiana curtseyed but did not meet Elizabeth's eyes.

"You must call me Elizabeth, or even Lizzy." Elizabeth approached and laid a hand on the younger girl's arm. "I am pleased to have you as a new sister."

Georgiana smiled and met Elizabeth's eyes at last. She had wanted to convey to the younger girl that she was pleased with all she knew of her and would not love her only for Darcy's sake.

Soon, they were inside and refreshing from their journey before a family dinner planned by Georgiana. As the evening wore on, Elizabeth's gentle patience with the girl was rewarded. Georgiana increasingly left her shyness and timidity behind. They talked mostly of music and discussed duets they could practise in the coming weeks.

Elizabeth also conversed easily with Mrs. Annesley, and a scheme began to brew in her mind. Georgiana was not alone in her struggles. Too often Society would not even care about the causes for her troubles and condemn her as mad before packing her away to an asylum. There were others like Jane. Surely there were even more like Elizabeth. She had never contemplated suicide, but she had been in just as much pain and felt just as lost. She knew she needed help but had nowhere to turn. How she needed the bright light of compassion from someone! She would spend the rest of her life thanking God that Darcy came to illuminate her way.

She had not known how she would fill her time once she came to Pemberley, but as the evening wore on, Elizabeth considered a profound thought. If she could find others willing to be a beacon of hope, they would not be a small and distant light as dim as a candle. Instead, they would be a torch aflame for all to see. She knew no one, save the people in Pemberley's music room and relatives who had abandoned her or were too stubborn to admit their need. Elizabeth could change that, though. She had always been gifted in the art of conversation. This shared goal would be a quality she looked for when making new friends. Surely she would meet Darcy's neighbours, and eventually they would go to London. She was not as confident as he that there was no good to be found in the *ton*.

As Elizabeth ended her first day as mistress of Pemberley in her husband's arms, she sighed in happiness. She had found the love of her life and perhaps the reason for her struggles. She would use them to help others. Georgiana could never replace her sisters, but she offered something even better: a sibling relationship built out of genuine love and respect and not merely the ties of blood. Soon, there would be letters from Longbourn, as well as news of Kitty and Lydia. She would decide how to reply to them when the time came. However, Elizabeth was determined never to be guilted or manipulated again. Despite it all, she could forgive, and even be grateful for, Mrs. Bennet. For without the woman's destructive parenting, Elizabeth never would have met Darcy once more or learned the most valuable lesson of loving herself.

Epilogue

Ten years later

Darcy smiled politely as person after person entered his London house. Beside him, Elizabeth greeted each guest with a charming smile and welcomed them to their home. This evening, they hosted prospective trustees of the London branch of the Society for the Preservation of Feminine Talent. Elizabeth had named the organisation thus so as not to garner anger at the idea of encouraging independence for ladies while also not infantilising them.

The foundation formed shortly after their marriage and served the Lambton area first. Eventually, Elizabeth took the idea to influential members of urban populations such as Manchester and Birmingham. Last year, they opened a branch in Liverpool. Expansion to London would be their most extensive yet. Of course, quite a bit of the notoriety belonged to the influence of the former Miss Angelina Maria Lucks.

Shortly after arriving at Pemberley, Darcy had sent his solicitor to confirm from Miss Lucks that she was indeed Lydia Bennet. She admitted her real identity, but desired no assistance from the Darcys and planned to take the London stage by storm with hopes of marrying nobility. A few years ago, she married an aging lord who needed a new countess after his wife's death bearing their fifth son. At first there was still no connection to the Darcys. However, a political rival of her husband dug up proof of Lydia's fallen status. Society, in general, did not think well of actresses, but Lydia had managed discretion in any affairs she had. The supposed proof, however, was not from Lydia's time with an acting troupe in Scotland or her elopement with the still-at-large George Wickham. No, someone had visited the South Mimms Inn in Hertfordshire and swore there was once a serving lady who called herself Lizzy Smith and looked just like the new Lady Randall. Lydia could have defended herself and lay the blame on her sister, but she never did. In turn, the extremely respectable Mrs. Darcy befriended the countess. Rather than taking lovers like most of the aristocratic ladies, Lydia had turned her activities towards charitable works after retiring from the stage. Between the two sisters, the Society garnered more attention than expected.

After dinner and the requisite separation of the sexes, Elizabeth took a moment to explain the purpose of the Society to the assembled guests.

"My good lords and ladies," Elizabeth said, "we meet this evening to discuss the founding of a new branch of the Society of Preservation of Feminine Talent. It is my belief that every woman has talents given to her at birth and are deserving of protection."

"Protection, you say?" an older man asked. "They ought to have fathers to protect them."

"I agree, sir," she answered. "However, some do not. Death is no respecter of persons. We may be at peace now, but war may come again, and disease is never far away. Additionally, not all men who bear children are capable of being responsible parents. Indeed, some abuse their wives and children."

The older gentleman harrumphed. "Then family ought to involve themselves."

"Again, sir, that is not always possible. The fact is, some ladies leave the protection of the homes to which they were born. What is she to do? Seek employment when she has no experience or training? The results of such a gamble are seldom in the lady's favour."

"What does the Society do, Mrs. Darcy?" a lady from the back asked.

"We do have ministers and physicians, but that is not all that is required to assist the ladies, and it is not always easy to find those services given by people with the desire to help and not condemn. The Society provides safe homes and healthy meals for our ladies. For the working classes, we teach them valuable skills which can lead to employment. For the gentry, we fill any gaps in their education and keep them immersed in proper society befitting their station. Most importantly, for both groups, we minister to the damaged psyche of our guests."

The old gentleman stood up and thumped his walking cane. "Are there not workhouses? Are there not churches? You reach beyond your scope, madam." He shuffled past the others and stood before Darcy. "Sir, you ought to call your wife to order."

"She has things well in order, sir, and I fully support her," Darcy replied.

Shaking his head, the gentleman exited the room and, Darcy had little doubt, the house as well. This portion was always the most difficult for him to watch. He could hardly conceive of anyone not finding his wife brilliant and was still her most steadfast supporter. In turn, during their ten years of marriage, Elizabeth had been there for him countless times, from the wrath of Lady Catherine to the unexpected death of his uncle Joseph, even to inheriting control of Rosings and all the strain of managing two estates after his cousin Anne's demise.

His eyes met Elizabeth's, but hers did not shine with tears of rejection. She stood erect, pausing to allow others a moment of decision before she continued. A few others excused themselves, but the vast majority remained. Whether they achieved their goal this night or not, Darcy could barely restrain his pride in his wife's confidence and courage.

"Now that we have that over with"—she smiled, and the crowd chuckled—"I wanted you to listen to the testimony of some of our ladies and other benefactresses."

Elizabeth ceded the floor and came to Darcy's side as three different women gave their stories. They ranged from as extreme as

Georgiana's experiences to as mild as Elizabeth's. The other patronesses spoke about the statistical data of the women they helped. The majority came from middle-class to lower-gentry families. They never turned away a working-class woman, but their primary goal had always been to help the women no one believed could have terrible families. Shocked gasps and disgusted mutterings rippled through the room when the final patroness explained that one in four of the ladies they helped, regardless of social class, had been sexually abused before adulthood.

Elizabeth had a final speech to close the presentation portion of the evening. Afterward, it would resume as any regular dinner party, and card tables would be brought out. In another room, ladies were welcome to exhibit on the pianoforte.

"Ladies and gentlemen," Elizabeth beseeched, "do not merely take our words on the matter. Visit our facility in Bloomington. We have not invited you here to raid your purses. Our Society is already well-funded and has established our newest location in a respectable neighbourhood, and with all we could need. The meaning behind this evening's presentation was purely educational. Now that you know of a need, I only ask what your compassion would have you do."

The crowd applauded, none heartier than Darcy. When she reached his side, he raised her hand to his lips. She still claimed his act of kindness had saved her, but all Darcy could think about was how many ladies she had saved in the years since.

Slowly, through years of patience and firm boundaries, they had resumed visitations with Jane and Mary. Mrs. Bennet had refused to ever accept any responsibility for matters but wrote civil letters, and they had seen her a few times while they visited the Gardiners, who had fully apologised to Elizabeth. Neither the Gardiners nor Mrs. Bennet were welcome at any Darcy property, but Elizabeth did not lack for company. She had found a faithful, steadfast sister in Georgiana, who while much healed had not yet married, and a loving relation in Darcy's paternal aunt Katherine Sneyd. Elizabeth had made many acquaintances via her work with the Society, and several of them were her bosom friends. She corresponded with friends in Ireland from their many visits to the island. Elizabeth also wrote to Mrs. Scott, the woman from their trip to Portpatrick, and her daughter in Glasgow. None of it surprised Darcy; he always knew Elizabeth would be well-loved.

After their guests left, Darcy escorted Elizabeth to their chamber. Holding her to his chest as they fell asleep, he considered then, as always, how thankful he was for finding her at the inn of a small Hertfordshire town. He could hardly fathom what life would have been like without her, but it certainly would not have included four bright-eyed children with Elizabeth's smile. Nor would Darcy have known the deep fulfillment one could have when assisting others. The most significant difference of all, of course, was that he would not have in his arms the woman he loved beyond all others and who completed his heart.

He had loved her then; now she was imperative to his life. Marrying Elizabeth was not an act of compassion. He had no more choice in the matter than he had in drawing breath into his lungs. She was the greatest gift he could ever conceive, and he would forever be grateful for the second chance which led him to find her.

The End

Author Note

The statistic about one in four women being sexually abused before adulthood is a contemporary number for residents of the United States. No figures were gathered during the Regency era or at all until recently. Nor is it a problem faced only by women. In fact, one in six boys is abused before they reach eighteen.

To learn more about these facts and how you can prevent sexual abuse toward the children in your life, I suggest looking at this site: https://defendinnocence.org/

*Although I am an independent presenter with Younqiue, I am not affiliated with The Younique Foundation or Defend Innocence. The contents of this book are not endorsed by Younique, The Younique Foundation, or Defend Innocence.

Acknowledgments

To my author friends Leenie and Zoe that always were willing to hold my hand, nothing can take your place in my heart. Thank you, Anna Horner for your invaluable editing skills.

Thank you to the countless other people of the JAFF community who have inspired and encouraged me.

Last but not least, I could never have written, let alone published, without the love and support of my beloved husband and babies!

About the Author

Born in the wrong era, Rose Fairbanks has read nineteenth-century novels since childhood. Although she studied history, her transcript also contains every course in which she could discuss Jane Austen. Never having given up all-nighters for reading, Rose discovered her love for Historical Romance after reading Christi Caldwell's Heart of a Duke Series.

After a financial downturn and her husband's unemployment had threatened her ability to stay at home with their special needs child, Rose began writing the kinds of stories she had loved to read for so many years. Now, a best-selling author of Jane Austen-inspired stories, she also writes Regency Romance, Historical Fiction, Paranormal Romance, and Historical Fantasy.

Having completed a BA in history in 2008, she plans to finish her master's studies someday. When not reading or writing, Rose runs after her two young children, ignores housework, and profusely thanks her husband for doing all the dishes and laundry. She is a member of the Jane Austen Society of North America and Romance Writers of America.

You can connect with Rose on Facebook,Instagram, Pinterest, and her blog: http://rosefairbanks.com

To join her email list for information about new releases and any other news, you can sign up here: http://eepurl.com/bmJHjn

Facebook fans! Join Rose's reading groups:

Rose's Reading Garden

Jane Austen Re-Imaginings Series

Christmas with Jane

When Love Blooms Series

Pride and Prejudice and Bluestockings Series

Loving Elizabeth Series

More by Rose Fairbanks

Jane Austen Re-Imaginings Series
(Stand Alone Series)
Letters from the Heart
Undone Business
No Cause to Repine
Love Lasts Longest
Mr. Darcy's Kindness
Mr. Darcy's Compassion

When Love Blooms Series
Sufficient Encouragement
Renewed Hope
Extraordinary Devotion

Loving Elizabeth Series
Pledged
Reunited
Treasured
Loving Elizabeth Collection (Books 1-3)

Pride and Prejudice and Bluestockings
Mr. Darcy's Bluestocking Bride
Lady Darcy's Bluestocking Club (Coming 2019)

Impertinent Daughters Series
The Gentleman's Impertinent Daughter
Mr. Darcy's Impertinent Daughter (Coming 2019)

Desire and Obligation Series
A Sense of Obligation
Domestic Felicity (Coming 2019)

Christmas with Jane
Once Upon a December
Mr. Darcy's Miracle at Longbourn
How Darcy Saved Christmas

Men of Austen
The Secrets of Pemberley
The Secrets of Donwell Abbey (*Emma* Variation, Coming 2019)

Regency Romance

Flowers of Scotland (Marriage Maker Series)
The Maid of Inverness

Paranormal Regency Fairy Tale
Cinderella's Phantom Prince and Beauty's Mirror (with Jenni James)

Printed in Great
Britain
by Amazon